"*The Odds* . . . offers a compelling window into the way that the 2008 economic collapse has affected the lives of average Americans."
—*The New Yorker* Book Bench

"[*The Odds*] keeps you on the edge of your seat through the 179 pages of this brisk, pungent journey into a marriage afflicted by the twenty-first century."
—*Pittsburgh Post-Gazette*

"The odds of the Fowlers reconciling should their marriage fail may be slim (1 in 20,480 that a divorced couple will remarry), but the odds that O'Nan will write winsome fiction—be it long or short-form—are forever high."
—*St. Louis Post-Dispatch*

"*The Odds* is a remarkable portrait of a marriage stressed to the breaking point, a husband and wife united and divided by bad luck and their own thorny history. This slender, moving book confirms O'Nan's status as one of the best writers of his generation, a novelist who can illuminate the drama and complexity of everyday life with compassion, wry humor, and unflinching honesty."
—Tom Perrotta, *New York Times* bestselling author of *The Leftovers*

"Stewart O'Nan once drove me too fast through Manhattan at 3 AM. This book feels just like that. Dangerous, domestic, sad, thrilling, slyly hilarious, and painful. It's a love song, yes, but a love song to a dying marriage. Read it, please."
—Sherman Alexie, National Book Award–winning author of *War Dances*

"Stewart O'Nan is a novelist of the everyday. . . . *The Odds* . . . concerns people you might run into at Target. . . . O'Nan packs his granular observations about domestic life into a smart, fast-paced romantic-comedy format. . . . Call it *Bonnie and Clyde* meets the old Albert Brooks' film *Lost in America*. . . . What's portrayed especially well, even in the farcical circumstances, is the everyday negotiations, internal and interpersonal, governing the spouses' lives: their calculations of what to say when, and how. . . . [It's] a funny book, too. . . . O'Nan even grants his characters (and readers) that the cheap magic of a tourist trap like Niagara Falls can be magic, nonetheless."
—*Pittsburgh City Paper*

"*The Odds* is a realistic fairy tale about the gravitational pull of an enduring relationship. In deft, knowing strokes, Stewart O'Nan exposes all the tenderness and tension, the compromises and evasions that lie at the heart of any long-term marriage. . . . Anyone who's experienced those emotions and doesn't confess to seeing at least a cloudy reflection in the mirror O'Nan has so lovingly crafted isn't telling the truth." —*Shelf Awareness*

ABOUT THE AUTHOR

Stewart O'Nan is the author of thirteen novels, including *Snow Angels; A Prayer for the Dying; Last Night at the Lobster;* and *Emily, Alone.* He was born and raised and lives with his family in Pittsburgh.

To access Penguin Readers Guides online, visit our Web site at www.penguin.com.

THE ODDS

Stewart O'Nan

PENGUIN BOOKS

PENGUIN BOOKS
Published by the Penguin Group
Penguin Group (USA) Inc., 375 Hudson Street, New York, New York 10014, U.S.A. • Penguin
Group (Canada), 90 Eglinton Avenue East, Suite 700, Toronto, Ontario, Canada M4P 2Y3 (a division
of Pearson Penguin Canada Inc.) • Penguin Books Ltd, 80 Strand, London WC2R 0RL, En-
gland • Penguin Ireland, 25 St. Stephen's Green, Dublin 2, Ireland (a division of Penguin Books
Ltd) • Penguin Books Australia Ltd, 250 Camberwell Road, Camberwell, Victoria 3124, Australia
(a division of Pearson Australia Group Pty Ltd) • Penguin Books India Pvt Ltd, 11 Community
Centre, Panchsheel Park, New Delhi – 110 017, India • Penguin Group (NZ), 67 Apollo Drive,
Rosedale, Auckland 0632, New Zealand (a division of Pearson New Zealand Ltd) • Penguin Books
(South Africa) (Pty) Ltd, 24 Sturdee Avenue, Rosebank, Johannesburg 2196, South Africa

Penguin Books Ltd, Registered Offices: 80 Strand, London WC2R 0RL, England

First published in the United States of America by Viking Penguin,
a member of Penguin Group (USA) Inc. 2012
Published in Penguin Books 2012

10   9   8   7   6   5   4   3   2   1

Publisher's Note
This is a work of fiction. Names, characters, places, and incidents either are the product of the author's
imagination or are used fictitiously, and any resemblance to actual persons, living or dead, business
establishments, events, or locales is entirely coincidental.

THE LIBRARY OF CONGRESS HAS CATALOGED THE HARDCOVER EDITION AS FOLLOWS:
O'Nan, Stewart.
  The odds : a love story / Stewart O'Nan.
    p.   cm.
  ISBN 978-0-670-02316-5 (hc.)
  ISBN 978-0-14-312227-2 (pbk.)
  I. Title.
  PS3565.N316O33 2012
  813'.54—dc23
  2011033330

Printed in the United States of America
Designed by Carla Bolte • Set in Simoncini Garamond

The wheel of fortune
goes spinning round
Will the arrow point my way?
Will this be the day?
O wheel of fortune
don't pass me by
Let me know the magic of
a kiss and a sigh
While the wheel is spinning, spinning, spinning
I'll not dream of winning
fortune or fame
While the wheel is turning, turning, turning
I'll be ever yearning
for love's precious flame
O wheel of fortune
I'm hoping somehow
if you'll ever smile on me
please let it be now.

—*Dinah Washington*

The Odds

Odds of a U.S. tourist visiting Niagara Falls:

1 in 195

The final weekend of their marriage, hounded by insolvency, indecision, and, stupidly, half secretly, in the never-distant past ruled by memory, infidelity, Art and Marion Fowler fled the country. North, to Canada. "Like the slaves," Marion told her sister Celia. They would spend their last days and nights as man and wife as they'd spent the first, nearly thirty years ago, in Niagara Falls, as if, across the border, by that fabled and overwrought cauldron of new beginnings, away from any domestic, everyday claims, they might find each other again. Or at least Art hoped so. Marion was just hoping to endure it with some grace and get back home so she could start dealing with the paperwork required to become, for the first time in her life, a single-filing taxpayer.

They told their daughter Emma they were taking a second honeymoon.

"Plus they're doing another open house here, so . . ." Marion, on the other line, qualified.

They weren't good liars, they were just afraid of the truth and what it might say about them. They were middle-class, prey to the tyranny of appearances and what they could afford, or dare, which was part of their problem. They were too settled and practical for what they were doing, uncomfortable with desperate

1

measures. They could barely discuss the plan between themselves, as if, exposed to light and air, it might evaporate.

With Jeremy, it was enough to say they wanted to see the new casino, a Frank Gehry knockoff featured on the covers of Sunday travel sections and in-flight magazines. He was impressed with the rate they'd gotten. Art had dug around online to find a bargain.

"Your father the high roller," Marion joked.

The Valentine's Getaway Special, it was called: $249, inclusive of meals and a stake of fifty Lucky Bucks toward table games.

They took the bus because it was part of the package, but now, burrowing through a dark wind tunnel of blowing snow somewhere on the outskirts of Buffalo, surrounded by much younger couples—including, frozen zoetropically in the light of oncoming cars, a fleshy pair in Harley gear necking directly across the aisle—they both wished they'd driven.

They'd already made their separate cases at home, so there was no sense going over it again. Art, ever the math major, always bringing matters back to the stingy reality of numbers, had pointed out it would save them fifty dollars in gas, not to mention parking, which Marion thought absurd, and typical. They were so far beyond the stage where fifty dollars might help—like this ridiculous gamble, betting their marriage, essentially, on the spin of a wheel—yet he clung to his old a-penny-saved-is-a-penny-earned bookkeeping, forgetting the ledger he was tending was drenched in red. Taking the bus represented yet another loss of control, giving themselves up to the hand of fate, or at least a sleep-deprived driver. The only reason she went along with it—besides not wanting to fight—was that she wouldn't have to worry about Art tailgating people the whole way in this weather, though of course she didn't say that.

The bus, additionally, was supposed to provide them with cover, as if in gray middle age they weren't invisible enough. From the beginning Art had conceived of the trip as a secret mission, a fantastic last-ditch escape from the snares of their real life, and while Marion refused to believe in the possibility, as at first she'd refused to believe the severity of their situation, she also knew they'd run out of options. The house had been on the market over a year now without a nibble. They would lose it— had already lost it, honestly. The question was, how much would it cost them?

Everything, barring a miracle. Art had already crunched the numbers, and after a necessary period of denial, Marion had conceded them, which was why they were barreling north on I-90, Lake Erie a black void beyond the window.

Art just wanted to get there. The Indians gym bag on his lap with the leering, bucktoothed Chief Wahoo made him nervous, as if the banded packets of twenties fitted inside like bricks were stolen. He wouldn't be able to relax until he'd locked them in the safe, along with the ring he'd managed to keep a secret from Marion. In love he wasn't frugal, despite what she might say. In another mad surrender to extravagance, for seventy-five more dollars a night, he'd reserved one of the bridal suites on the top floor overlooking the Falls, and despite their guaranteed late arrival, he was afraid the front desk might have lost or ignored his request and given their room away.

Beside him, Marion lowered her mystery and massaged her neck as if she had a crick in it.

"I'm starving," she said. "Aren't you hungry?"

It was the only bus of the day, but since he'd made the arrangements he was responsible, just as it was his fault the traffic was bad and the weather ugly, and that night had fallen.

"I'm a little peckish," he seconded. As in everything this weekend, he wanted them to be on the same side, the two of them against the world.

"What time is our reservation?"

"The earliest I could get was seven-thirty."

"What time is it now?"

"Just past six. It's only another twenty miles."

"I should have grabbed a breakfast bar. I still need to iron my dress. I hope they have one."

"They should."

"Should be like a wood bee," she said.

It was a private joke, a mocking appreciation of the slipperiness of even the simplest hope, a nonce catchphrase like so many others lifted from favorite movies or TV shows that served as a rote substitute for conversation and bound them like shut-in twins, each other's best and, most often, only audience. While they'd performed this exchange hundreds of times over the years, en route to graduations, weddings and funerals, and her skepticism was an old routine, delivered lightly, almost without thought, tonight, because he was on a mission to recapture, by one dashing, reckless gesture everything they'd lost, he took it personally. He liked to believe that when he first met her, when she was completely foreign and even more inscrutable, a solemn blonde sociology major freshly graduated from Wooster with granny glasses and a tennis player's shapely legs, a girlish love of James Taylor and Dan Fogelberg, a cedar chest full of pastel sweaters and a shelf crowded with naked neon-haired troll dolls, she had believed in things—luck, goodness, the inexhaustible possibilities of life—and that her disappointment now was a judgment not of the world but of him and their life together. If the room didn't have an iron, he would call down to the front desk and go get it himself if necessary. They might be broke come Monday morning, and filing for divorce, but he would never stop trying to provide for her happiness, as impossible as that was.

She addressed her mystery again, tilting it to the beam of light from the overhead console. She read two or three a week, the pile of cracked and yellowing paperbacks on her nightstand dwindling as the one on the marble-topped table by the front door grew until it was time to trade them in at the Book Exchange. "I'm reading," she'd say when his hand was advancing under the covers, and he would retreat.

Across the aisle, in flickering montage, the biker couple clutched at each other like plummeting skydivers, and Art was aware of the space separating him from her. He slipped his hand from atop the gym bag and dropped it to her blue-jeaned thigh, a middle-school move. He squeezed the yielding loaf of her leg, smoothed, patted. It had been weeks since they'd made love, and the last time had been a disappointment, perfunctory on her part, workmanlike on his. He'd had to lobby her for it, imagining ecstasy, the two of them communing, the sweet plenty of her body wiping his mind clean of worry, and then, in the middle, it felt like a chore, and he'd struggled to finish, grudgingly picturing the overly rouged girl who did the traffic on the morning news. Tonight, with the Falls roaring below their window, he would prove that while they'd reached the age where passion sometimes flagged, his love for her was as strong as ever. Didn't she see? The money, the house, none of it mattered. Since they'd met, with the exception of those few torturous months he'd long since repudiated, she was all he wanted. Mawkish as it sounded, he could say it with a straight face: as long as they had each other, they were rich.

Marion stayed his hand, covering it with her own, and kept reading. With nowhere to focus his attention, he was always needy on vacation, just as he'd been following her around the house all fall since he'd lost his job. He was eager—too eager, really—and normally she could divert him with a list of chores. She put him in charge of the leaves, checking on him surreptitiously from the bathroom window as she would Emma and Jeremy when they were teenagers, glad to have an hour to herself. One of her worries about this weekend was how much time they would spend alone together. At home she could busy herself running errands and making supper, messing around on Facebook and watching TV, and hide behind her mystery in bed. Here he would want more of her, as if this really was a second honeymoon.

To her it was the exact opposite. With every passing mile she was returning to a place where thirty years ago she'd been a different and certainly a better person—if naïve and a bit silly, then relatively untouched by the larger sorrows of life, several of which, later on, were the result of her own decisions, choosing desire over duty only to discover she was wrong about everything, including who she was. The idea of that younger, blameless Marion chastened her, as if once they arrived she would have to meet with her and formally review her regrets once more.

She didn't care about the money. She was sad about the house, and sorry for Art, but the children were gone and they could live anywhere. Secretly, as horrible as it sounded, she was actually looking forward to moving into a smaller place and starting over, or so she told herself, because sometimes, alone in the car at a stoplight or on the toilet with the door closed, she was subject to moments of trancelike blankness, staring straight ahead at nothing while biting the inside of one cheek as if trying to solve an impossible problem.

She wasn't in love with him, or not the way she thought she should be. She wasn't in love with Karen anymore, if she'd ever really been. She wasn't in love with anyone, especially not herself. At some point, after menopause had robbed her of that bodily need, she'd convinced herself that the great movements in her life were in the past and succumbed to the inertia of middle age—prematurely, it seemed. While Art saw the divorce as a legal formality, a convenient shelter for whatever assets they might have left, from the beginning she'd taken the idea seriously, weighing her options and responsibilities—plumbing, finally, her heart—trying, unsuccessfully, to keep the ghost of Wendy Daigle out of the equation.

How much easier it would be if Wendy Daigle was dead. But

Wendy Daigle wasn't dead. Against every reasonable measure of justice, Wendy Daigle was living with her second husband in Lakewood, just the other side of Cleveland, on a cul-de-sac, in a tan raised ranch with an aboveground pool in the backyard and a homemade hockey net in the driveway. Their e-mail and phone were unlisted, but Marion had the license number of her Suburban written in tiny print at the bottom of the very last page of her old address book, where, occasionally, it would remind her of what a fool Art had thought she was.

She'd lost her spot on the page and read the same sentence again, sighed and kneaded the bunched muscles of her neck.

"Want a neck rub?" Art offered.

"I'm just tired of sitting." She shifted and went back to her book, ignoring him again.

These little rebuffs, he would never get used to them. Years ago he'd come to accept that no matter how saintly he was from then on, like a murderer, he would always be wrong, damned by his own hand, yet he was always surprised and hurt when she turned him down. Gently, perhaps, but flatly, straight to his face, dismissing him as if he were a servant, his assistance no longer needed. As he was telling himself he had no right to feel slighted, his glance lighting on, then flitting away from the biker couple, from the front of the bus came a bang like a bomb going off—his first thought not a car but that phantom bugaboo, terrorists—the seismic impact jerked them forward, and, sickeningly, as if on a pivot, the entire rear end began to slide, and then, as the driver overcorrected, trying to bring it back, broke loose.

Odds of being killed in a bus accident:

  1 in 436,212

"Hang on!" someone behind them yelled, as a laptop clattered to the floor.

Marion grabbed at him, her book already gone, while he threw his arms straight out to brace himself against the seat back. The driver braked, and the gym bag flew across the aisle, bouncing around the bikers' shins like a loose fumble. For a second Art thought of extricating himself from her grip to fall on it, but—just as quick—saw the problem with that option, and waited, rigid, still braced for impact, as the bus slowed, then stopped.

"What the hell."

Marion relinquished her grip. "Sorry."

"It's all right."

"I don't think that was part of the deluxe package."

"No."

"Is everyone all right?" a woman up front asked.

"No," an older woman answered calmly.

The gym bag lay on its side in the aisle, safely zipped. As he bent forward, stretching to retrieve it, the biker guy reached down, picked it up by one handle and passed it to him.

"Go Tribe."

Art blanked, then caught up. "You know it. Thanks."

"Whatta ya got in there—bricks?"

"Ha!"

Outside, copper-tinted snow blew through the high lights. They were sideways across all three lanes, the stopped traffic behind them cockeyed like bumper cars when the ride ends.

Up front, the driver was checking on the woman who wasn't all right. Across the aisle, people were collecting their possessions, craning at their windows, calling on their cellphones. Gradually news filtered back. It wasn't a car. A U-Haul trailer had gotten loose and run into them, or they'd run into it. There were clothes all over the road. The biker concluded—unhelpfully, Art thought—that they weren't going anywhere for a while.

"Great." Marion held up her book by its flimsy cover, the pages butterflied. "I lost my place."

Sitting there with the bag as she flipped the pages, he allowed himself to think of all the problems it would have solved if the bus had rolled and he alone had been killed. How clean it would be. No one could call it suicide, and Marion would receive the full half-million benefit, more than enough to pay off their debts. The policy had been in place forever, so no one would suspect. It was true that more than a few times over the last year he'd imagined his own death, though he would deny he'd ever been suicidal. He preferred to think of himself as practical rather than depressed, so that even now he viewed the crash as a missed opportunity, like a crime he wasn't quite skilled or steely enough to pull off. He suspected there was something wanting in him to think like this, some lack of courage or integrity. His life had been staid and sedate for the most part, yet now that he was being tested, he grasped at the most dire solutions.

With a blip of static the driver came on the intercom and announced there would be a delay. He'd already called dispatch; a replacement bus was en route. He apologized for the inconvenience.

"Just what I want to do," Marion said, "get on another bus."

"Hmp," Art snorted, to let her know she'd landed the joke, and that at heart he agreed. She went back to her book. As a complaint it was a mild one, delivered wryly, and well-deserved. He was hungry too, and tired. He understood that she didn't want to be there, that this was just another ludicrous episode in the worst year of their lives—or possibly the second worst—and yet, while it was probably just a reflex, he was happy that, literally in the face of death, of all the possible reactions she might have had, she'd reached for him and hung on.

Odds of a vehicle being searched by Canadian customs:

   1 in 384

   The Peace Bridge was lit up like a carnival ride, its trusses bathed a gaudy purple. Below the road deck, red navigation beacons warned boaters away from the great stone piers, tinting the dark river, making Marion think of all the freezing water headed for the Falls. It might beat them, depending on how long they had to wait at the tollbooths. He'd called and changed their reservation so they weren't late, but after the delay, and changing buses, she was impatient.

   Their first time they'd crossed during the day, a steamy Sunday in June, the two of them alone in his old Corolla, their friends' squiggly shaving cream letters dried on the side windows. Just married—it was hard to recall the feeling, though she could see herself in her favorite white linen sundress, showing off her new ring to the customs agent. The idea made her wistful for that time before everything, the two of them younger than their children were now.

   She'd been doing foster care in Cleveland and met him at a farewell party for a fellow caseworker who'd had enough of the revolving door of family court.

   He was one of just a few men there, and the only one in a suit, having come directly from the office. He was tall, with broad shoulders like a football player, but had the gangly, near-concave leanness of a boy. The bridge of his nose was generously freckled, his hair a lank cinnamon brown, a little long for her taste, and from time to time as they spoke he had to dip his head to one side and swipe it out of his eyes. He wrote grant proposals for Children's Hospital downtown. His newest was for a mobile pediatric clinic—basically a tricked-out Winnebago—that would visit low-income neighborhoods on a rotating basis. In an effort to impress her, he was overly enthusiastic, as if he was on a crusade to fix the city. She wasn't so cruel as to tell him it couldn't be done. As he was describing its monthly route, ticking off names of notorious housing projects where she regularly did home visits with her clients, he threw one arm wide, sloshing beer out of his cup in a liquid arc that fell splashing to the hardwood floor. Before she could stop herself, she let loose a whoop of a laugh, drawing the whole room's attention, and to her astonishment, the overgrown boy in the suit before her blushed deeply, red-cheeked as a leprechaun.

"I'm glad you think I'm funny."

"I'm glad you're funny," she said.

Their courtship lasted more than a year, but in that moment she had already chosen—wrongly, it turned out, at least in one important category, which made it that much harder, now, stuck in the bus, to recall the happiness she'd felt then. Her entire life had not been a ruin. There were seasons she'd keep, years with the children, days and hours with Art and, yes, despite the miserable end, with Karen. Vacations, special occasions. The patients she'd come to love and then learned to let go. She'd be damned if she'd let Wendy Daigle poison everything.

BRIDGE ICES BEFORE ROAD, a sign advised, and they motored up a swooping approach and onto the span itself, suspended, briefly, between the two countries. Snow swirled purple through the superstructure. Earlier they'd both filled out declarations swearing they weren't bringing any produce or plants or potentially damaging insects or animals into the country, or more than ten thousand dollars Canadian. Legally, he said, you were allowed to bring in as much as you wanted. The crime was not reporting it. The law was really about money laundering and funding terrorism, not what they were doing. Most likely they wouldn't be searched anyway, being part of a tour. His blitheness disturbed her, as if once again he'd become that other person, the one who would say or do anything to get what he wanted. Did he understand how hard it was to believe a word he said when he lied so easily?

Spotlit flags flapped atop the tollbooths. As she remembered it, the plaza was smaller, and there was no modern-looking glass cube in the middle, no fancy rock fountain. They angled their way past the lines of stopped cars to an empty lane dedicated to buses. As they slowed for the jersey-walled slot, he shoved the bag under the seat in front of him, sliding a foot on either side. He raised his eyebrows and gave her a clownish grimace, as if he knew how useless this was.

They stopped, the bus releasing a pneumatic hiss, and the cabin lights snapped on. The door opened, letting in a few flakes, and a customs agent in a baseball cap with an embroidered gold badge climbed the stairs. He conferred with the driver, jotting something on his clipboard, then turned to the passengers. He filled the aisle, blocking any escape. The bus went silent, await-ing instructions. Marion couldn't tell if he had a gun, but he was fit. She pictured him tackling Art, their bags ransacked, the money confiscated. They would lose it all anyway, but, after everything, to never have that chance, slim as it was, seemed wrong. Was that how he rationalized what they were doing? Because, for the first time, she could see it.

"Welcome to Canada, folks," the agent said. "We're going to ask you to disembark for just a couple of minutes. Please have your passports and customs forms available for inspection."

They filed off, braving the cold for a moment, then standing in a switchbacked line in a bright office. The agents here were hatless and sat behind high counters like bank tellers.

An agent waved them up together and inspected their pass-ports. "Where are you coming from today?"

She let Art answer, nodding confirmation.

What was the purpose of their visit? What hotel were they staying at? Did they have anything to declare?

She waited for Art to stumble over the last one, but he just shook his head as if the question was moot. "Nothing."

"Enjoy your stay." The agent gave Art back both of their pass-ports, and they went outside and got on the bus again.

The bag was still there.

"That's terrible," he said. "They didn't even stamp our pass-ports."

"You want to go back?"

"No, but . . . I kind of wanted a Canada stamp. I don't have one yet."

"Okay, settle down," she said, because he was too pleased with himself.

"I'm just saying."

"And I'm just saying."

They let it rest there, a stalemate, but as they rode along, the lights whipping past beside her, she realized they were actually going to do this, that there was nothing stopping them, and had to admit she felt an illicit thrill, as if they'd gotten away with something.

Odds of a U.S. citizen being an
  American Express cardholder:

  1 in 10

The driver took them in via the scenic route, curving with the river, the rapids adding to the suspense. On the American side, disembodied headlights glided through the night. Somewhere on the dark water separating them bobbed a line of buoys beyond which rescue was unlikely if not impossible. Art kept this information to himself, watching for the first glimpse of the Falls. Ahead, an orange halo rose from the city, silhouetting a long black lump.

"Is that Goat Island there?" he prompted.

"I hope so. I'm ready to jump out of my skin."

"It must be," he said, because just ahead he could see a pink column of mist boiling up, spritzing the windows, turning the streetlights blurry. The river surged, sluicing ice chunks past snow-topped rocks, throwing off foam. Beneath the dieseling of the bus, subtle at first, then insistent, came a deeper rumbling, as of a great engine. The tremor grew to a muted roaring, enveloping them like the mist, vibrating in his chest as if the whole earth were shaking, and then, in an instant, the river dropped away to reveal the famous panorama, a mile wide, colored blood-red for the weekend.

Oooo, everyone said.

Marion had turned to the window. He leaned across, nestling against her back as if to get a better view, taking in the warmth and scent of her neck. He thought of wrapping his arms around her, but resisted, afraid of ruining the moment. Often when he was trying to be affectionate she accused him of just wanting to cop a feel, as if he were a teenager. The charge hurt worse because he was at least partly guilty. He'd always loved to touch her. He'd thought it was a compliment, his ardency, but somehow, now, it was a burden for her to be desired.

"Why do they have to do that?" she said. "Why can't they just have moonlight on it?"

"I think it's supposed to be fun."

"I guess I'm no fun then."

"I think you're fun."

"It's all right," she said softly. "I know what I am."

Had he said anything like that? He was baffled at how quickly they'd gone from riffing to these recriminations, as if she'd set a trap he'd been dumb enough to blunder into again. As always, not knowing what the problem was, he traced her unhappiness back to Wendy, for which he took full blame, though, after so many years, he thought they'd both suffered enough, a judgment he wisely kept private and which made him all the more guilty and unable to answer her. The safest response he could offer was silence.

"God, stop with the poo-poo face," she said. "It's fine, I just need to eat something."

He forgot about holding her and accepted this as his quest, as if it were a solution, not an excuse.

They were nearly there. The hotel rose directly opposite Bridal Veil Falls, the sinuous aluminum facade meant to resemble the cataract, the casino at its base a muscular whirlpool flinging off huge fanciful water droplets outlined in aqua neon. The bus pulled up the circular drive and as a group they tramped through the spongily carpeted lobby, open to the casino floor, manic with the jangling of slot machines.

Another tour had just arrived, so they had to wait. They stood in line like conscripts, minutes of their lives ticking away. Marion took out her book.

GAMBLING PROBLEM? a state-sanctioned poster asked. CALL 1-800-GAMBLER.

"We can go grab something and come back," he suggested.

"That's not what you want to do. Let's just stick with the plan."

The front desk hadn't lost their reservation, as he feared. The receptionist had them down for a nonsmoking Fallsview suite on the top floor with a queen-sized bed. All she needed was an imprint of a credit card.

He'd booked the room with his American Express, and handed it to her, watched her swipe it briskly through the machine. Technically, since he had no intention of paying the bill, he was guilty of fraud, or could be once he filed for bankruptcy, but that was months away, and by then so many other charges would have accumulated that the trustee assigned to his case would rightly assume he'd mismanaged his finances so badly that, owing alimony and with a piddling income, he was forced to use his credit cards to live. The debt would be forgiven, discharged with no more serious repercussion than he would never again own an American Express card.

"There you go," the receptionist said, holding it out between two fingers.

On its face, by his name, in a masterstroke promoting brand loyalty, the raised date reminded him that he'd been a member since 1981, the same year they were married. It was possible he'd used it here then, and in a flash he saw a map of the world with all of their travels connected by dotted lines. England, Ireland, Hawaii. In the Florida Keys they drank rumrunners and made love on the beach, rinsing themselves in the warm shallows. How many flights had they charged to this card, how many meals?

The receptionist ripped off the slip. Somewhere in a windowless room he was on camera, flattening the receipt against the counter in lo-res black-and-white. Fearing whoever was watching could read his intentions, he took the pen she'd given him and signed his name.

"Will you need help with your bags?"

"No, we can handle them," he said, because they'd spent enough money they didn't have and he wanted to leave—which turned out to be hasty, and the wrong answer, because in the elevator Marion asked him why he couldn't have just paid the bellhop the five dollars.

Odds of a married couple reaching their
25th anniversary:

1 in 6

There were roses and champagne waiting for them, and a red-cellophane-wrapped fruit basket with a note from the management. The sitting room was modern, everything made of bent chrome and black leather, even the lamps. It was bigger than their own living room, the drapes open to show off the Falls, floodlit and hallowed far below like an empty stage. Art went ahead, finding the lights, pointing out the amenities as if he were selling her a condo. There was a second flat-screen TV in the bedroom, a glass-walled shower stall and a huge jacuzzi for a tub. She didn't know whether to be impressed or upset by such opulence. She reminded herself that people stayed at much more luxurious places all the time.

"Check it out," he said, pulling a blind aside. "A tub with a view."

"That's great. Did you see an iron anywhere?"

He left her to search the bathroom cabinets, a minute later called from the hallway, "Got it!"

He came in beaming, holding it up like a prize. "It was in the closet."

"Thanks."

"You're welcome," he said.

"Was there a board?"

"I didn't see one."

"They wouldn't have an iron without a board."

She checked, and of course, in the same closet there was a small one hung from a bracket. "It's okay," she called. "I've got it."

He was hunched on one corner of the bed with the gym bag, trying to figure out the safe.

"Do you have anything you want me to iron?"

"Just a shirt."

What if she hadn't asked? He would have worn it wrinkled. He was like a teenager, or a bum, he honestly didn't care what he wore, never had. There were jackets in his closet from before Emma was born, resoled shoes he refused to throw out.

He fetched the shirt—a boring white oxford, though for years she'd tried to give his wardrobe some color. From habit, she did it first.

"Here you go." She held it out for him to take. "What are you going to do when I die?"

It was an old favorite. From her tone Art knew she was kidding, but it was a routine he hated, not merely for its hidden threat and insinuation of helplessness but also because the literal answer was forbidden. He could not say he would live. Sometimes, after too much wine, she would answer herself: "I don't know why I bother worrying. You'll be fine. You'll go marry your precious Wendy or some other young chick who'll take care of you." Which—though it had once, if only briefly, been the plan—had been rendered moot for so long it was painful to contemplate the idea that he'd risked losing everyone close to him for someone who turned out, after everything, to be a stranger to him, just as that former, lovestruck Art now seemed crazy. Equally insane was the notion that any young woman would be interested in a broke fifty-two-year-old with thinning hair, but that was never addressed. No, the real answer, the real reason the question tortured him, was that without Marion he wouldn't know what to do or even who he was. He could send his laundry out, but he would belong to that legion of aging, unloved men buying frozen dinners and six-packs at the grocery store, or, worse, working there, bagging their sad purchases and wishing them a good evening.

"Thank you," he said, trying to sound sufficiently grateful. "Don't let me forget, we need to change some of this money later. We shouldn't do it all at once."

"Right."

He still had to unpack, but took advantage of her being busy, and with a quick glance over his shoulder, snuck the silver gift-wrapped box with her ring from the bag and hid it deep in the safe, walling it in with stacks of twenties. Thankfully it all fit. Following the instructions inside the door, he changed the combination to her birthday, made sure it worked, then closed it again, congratulating himself in advance for arranging this surprise.

The ring was one more thing they couldn't afford but which, given their circumstances, would ultimately cost them nothing. After he filed, a trustee would go back and search for obvious large transfers to family members of money or property, like cars or second homes, which could then be retroactively seized. Not so with personal items, which were exempt up to ten thousand. It wasn't a tough choice. He'd much rather spend the money to make her happy than let the bank take it. Her original ring was modest, the best a young underwriter could do at the time. Now, with nothing left to save for, he was able to buy one that would make her cry. His plan was to surprise her with it Sunday night at dinner, both as a Valentine's gift and proof that, win or lose, he would always love her.

"What time is our new reservation?" she asked, laying out her dress.

"Eight-thirty. I doubt they're going to be very busy."

"You never know. It's Friday night."

For the overall sprawl of the suite, the bedroom was small. They changed on opposite sides of the bed, trying to stay out of each other's way, a ballet of accommodation. One of the great privileges of his life was watching her undress. Countless times she had asked him not to. It made her self-conscious, and lately she hadn't been happy with her body. Being less critical—being a man—he didn't understand. He'd always been happy with it, and now, discreetly, he appreciated the way she shed her jeans and top and, demurely facing away from him as she freed and then fitted their hooks, switched to a different bra. Rather than feeling deprived, he found her shyness girlish and endearing. Perhaps it was familiarity, but he thought her back one of her best features.

There was only one sink in the bathroom. She did her makeup, leaning into the mirror, and again he had to resist the urge to take her in his arms.

"What do you need?" she asked. "You're hovering."

"Just you."

She pretended to gag on a finger, sticking out her tongue.

"It's true. Plus I need to brush my teeth."

"You should have said so. I can move."

"No rush," he said, though they were going to be late.

He had to wait for her to choose a pair of earrings, a necklace, and finally a bracelet, in each case asking his opinion and then going with her own choice.

"Is there room in there for my jewelry bag?" she asked, and he knelt to tuck it away in the safe, glad to be able to do something for her.

On the way out, he made sure he had a room key.

"You look nice," she said at the elevators, plucking a long blonde hair from his lapel.

"Thank you, so do you."

"I'm sorry we didn't have time for a glass of champagne."

"Maybe in the tub later?"

She shushed him silently, pop-eyed, a finger to her lips, as if someone might be listening.

"Be a shame to waste that view."

"We'll see." Which could mean any number of things.

He clapped and rubbed his hands together like a silver screen villain. "So you're telling me there's a chance."

"Not if you act like that."

So he stopped.

Odds of getting sick on vacation:

    1 in 9

She always ordered the wrong thing—not because she didn't know her own tastes but because so often the descriptions were misleading. In the case of the monkfish, there was no mention of walnuts, which, though not allergic, she refused to eat, and had ever since she was a child. The bitter taste made her think of the castor oil her mother forced on her when she was sick, its emetic effect, and the chipped and swollen pressboard toilet seat in their old bathroom.

Art, as always, offered to trade with her. Already he was reaching his heavy plate over their wineglasses, his other hand open to take hers.

"Are you sure? You love tuna."

"I can get tuna anytime."

"Thank you," she said. "That's very giving of you."

"That's because I'm a giving person."

"That is true, you are." Sometimes too giving. Passive himself, he took up the causes of others with a tireless determination, whether it meant acting as treasurer for the parents' association trying to raise money for a new track at the high school or helping Mrs. Khalifa put together her satellite dish. Marion used this willingness against him to get things done around the house. Left to himself, he'd lie on the couch and watch football all weekend, but once motivated, he couldn't stop until the job, no matter how large, was done. He was more compulsive than impulsive, a plodder and a planner, not at all spontaneous, which was at least partly why she'd been so surprised he'd cheated on her, and why, though she hated him for it, deep inside she mostly blamed Wendy. He would have never done something like that on his own.

The tuna was perfectly cooked, the center the color of watermelon, with the jellied consistency of aspic. The wasabi–black pepper crust added a sinus-tingling bite she quelled with a slug of wine. "You sure you don't want this back? It's delicious—nice and rare."

"This is good too. It's a nice place." He gestured to the Falls across the gorge, endlessly pouring. "I'm surprised it's so empty."

"That might have something to do with the prices."

"This is the cheap one! This is like Burger King compared to the one on Sunday."

"After Sunday, Burger King's about all we'll be able to afford."

"After Sunday, Burger King is where we'll be working."

"To Burger King," she proposed.

"To Burger King." They clinked and drank. "You know, I don't think Burger King is hiring."

"Okay," she said, "let's talk about something else."

"Tomorrow night we've got Heart."

"You've gotta have Heart. When is that?"

"That's at eight, so dinner's early, at six. I was thinking we might do the fun stuff in the afternoon, depending what the weather's like. I don't know if Clifton Hill is open Sunday."

"I haven't seen a forecast."

"We definitely want to see the Ripley's Museum."

"*We*," she said.

"What, you don't?"

"I'd rather see a real museum."

"This is Niagara Falls, nothing's real here."

The waiter came over to check on them, restoring decorum. Did they want another bottle of the Chardonnay?

Art looked to her.

"I just want another glass." She'd already had three and was feeling them.

"Two glasses," Art said.

He rarely drank with her. It was nice. He could be attentive when he wanted to, and intimate, giving her his full concentration, turning their exchanges into flirty wordplay. The first intimation that things had gone wrong between them was the sudden absence of that easy, dancelike banter. He'd come home from work and be pleasant with the children and helpful in the kitchen, would read or watch TV like usual, but with her he was impersonal and bland, afraid to say anything in their private language for fear of lying. Later, she was the same way when she was carrying Karen around in her head, except that he never noticed. Or was it that she'd known Karen wasn't serious, that they'd been wrong from the start, the assumptions that brought them together—as Celia suggested—false at bottom, whereas he and Wendy Daigle were meant to be together?

"Damn it," she said.

"What?"

"Nothing."

"You're making your uh-oh face."

"I'm having bad thoughts."

"Don't have bad thoughts."

"I'm not trying to, I can't help it."

"Are you still going to have bad thoughts when we're divorced?"

"Why wouldn't I?"

"I thought it might work like bankruptcy, everything forgiven."

"Sorry, some debts you have to pay."

"It was worth a try," he said.

"Not really."

He'd finished her monkfish, leaving a slick of walnut pesto.

"You want the rest of this?" she asked. "It's delicious but I'm stuffed."

"Ask for a doggie bag. You can have it for a midnight snack."

"I don't think I'm going to be awake then. And I'm definitely not going to be hungry."

The waiter returned to clear and to see if he could tempt them with coffee or dessert. No, they were ready to go. They sipped their wine and watched the Falls, the few other couples ranked along the window. She envied them, assuming their lives, though no less complicated, must be happier, at least tonight.

The waiter came back and wished them a good evening. He hoped they would enjoy their stay.

"Thank you," she said when Art had paid the check.

"Thank American Express."

"It was nice."

"Good."

"I'm sorry I ruined it."

"You didn't ruin it," he said, subdued, helping her with her chair. He met her when she stood, and kissed her, holding her shoulders, rubbed the tops of her arms as if she were cold. "You've never ruined anything, so don't say you're sorry, okay?"

That was all she wanted, for him to fight for her. She was tired of being the wronged wife, the one he'd settled for out of guilt. Wasn't she worth winning? He'd never been jealous, even when he'd had good reason to be. He couldn't know what she'd ruined—to no purpose—proving she was still desirable, and her secret seemed monstrous and unfair. She misted up, overwhelmed, and held him.

"I'm sorry I'm sorry." Part of it was the wine, and part of it was that she was tired. She'd been angry for so long, she wanted him to feel the same way.

Standing there, holding her as if they were slow-dancing, Art wished he had the ring. The timing was right, the lights low, the room quiet. He would drop to one knee and offer himself to her. She would open the box and pull him up by his elbows, and the other couples would applaud. They would go upstairs and drink champagne, rechristen each other, giddy as newlyweds, and start fresh tomorrow.

Instead, on the way out, he grabbed her a peppermint, which she waved off with disgust, saying she'd eaten too much.

The mall they followed to the lobby was lined with upscale shops in which they were supposed to blow their winnings, though he assumed they were just for show—Tiffany, Louis

Vuitton, Swarovski, the Havana Tobacconist, even a Bentley dealership, outside of which sat a gleaming fastback, the grand prize in a raffle. Holding his hand, Marion paused at the Prada window to look over some leather coats. The mannequins were eyeless and inscrutable, all sleek cheekbones and pillowy lips. Now that the moment had passed, he wondered what magic words he'd uttered. He'd apologized, told her it was all his fault, but he'd been saying that ever since he confessed. It must have been something before that, but after the Bombay Sapphire and the wine he couldn't bring back their exact conversation.

It was common enough for her to bring up the subject on special occasions, as if she'd been waiting for the perfect moment, lobbing it into the middle of her birthday dinner or their anniversary. She had a genius for self-pity that defeated even his. He liked to believe that by act of will and the passage of time he'd gotten beyond thinking of Wendy every day, while Marion, who'd never met her, tended her memory like a widow.

Being eternally guilty, he was eternally defenseless against her, which fed a resentment he knew he wasn't entitled to, leaving him nothing with which to counter her anger but impatience and, after so long, exhaustion. Perhaps being sorry for being sorry meant that she knew she needed to let go but couldn't, out of wifely pride or simple spite. If so, the admission was a major shift, the recognition that they needed to change the way they were with each other if they were going to move on. Unless he was completely mistaken, she seemed to be asking for his help.

But he was not adept at reading her, especially after a few drinks. That had been made clear enough times in the past.

Approaching her with high spirits and what he thought were innocent hopes, he'd tasted more than his share of rejection, and he was wary. If she really was finally beginning to forgive him, he wouldn't risk it by pushing her.

Beside him, she made a queasy face, pressing a hand to her midsection as if she were having contractions. "How's your stomach?"

"Fine," he said.

"Mine's a little rumbly. Actually a lot rumbly."

"You're not going to throw up."

"I don't think so."

"I wonder if the tuna was bad."

"You had a few bites too."

"Not that many."

"It's probably just stress."

"We'll get you upstairs."

So no champagne. No tub. Now he was glad he didn't have the ring. He didn't want it associated with anything that could be read as a bad omen.

Let down, he turned calculating, scanning the lobby for a cashier's cage. Across from the elevators, the slot machines dinged and blinked, an empty temptation, their odds steeply tilted toward the house. Deeper within the casino, hidden somewhere among the acres of brightly patterned carpeting and table games, were two high-stakes French roulette wheels without the American model's unfair 00. He had hoped to locate them and stroll by to study the action before their dry run tomorrow night, but that, like so many other desires, would have to wait.

"Remember," she said, "you wanted to change that money."

"We can do it tomorrow."

"I'm fine, I think I just need to sit."

The elevator came and they took their positions against the rear wall, hoping no one would join them. To his relief, no one did. Normally when they were riding alone he would try to steal an inappropriate kiss—a game, since she was scandalized by cameras. Now, to show support, he held her hand.

In the hall, he went ahead to open the door for her. The turndown service had been in, leaving tempting breakfast menus for the doorknob and heart-shaped chocolates on their pillows. She dropped her purse on the bed and went directly to the bathroom. He pulled off his tie and stood looking at the view, a string of miniature streetlights describing a road on Goat Island. Beside it, the river ran invisible, fell red and frothing for a few seconds, shedding mist, then returned to darkness again. He and Wendy had poured champagne over each other, spent days barricaded in hotel rooms like fugitives, blinds drawn against the light. It was so long ago that he was tempted to cast those hours in a nostalgic haze, leaving out Marion completely. The great mystery to him wasn't the power of that happiness—he was at heart a romantic, and it was a romance—but how he could be so remorseless toward the rest of the world. Until then he'd thought of himself as a decent person. Afterwards he couldn't say what he was.

"Hey," Marion called.

"Is for horses."

"Can you hand me my book?"

"Where is it?"

It was waiting on her night table.

"Here you go. Oh my lord." Pinching his nose, he reached the mystery in to her and slapped on the fan.

"I know, I apologize. I think it was the tuna. And you feel fine."

"Strong like bull."

"Go do your money. I'm going to be a while."

"Want me to grab you some Gaviscon or something?"

"I don't think it would help. Maybe some Imodium."

"I'll see what they have."

The money was still there, just as he'd left it. Having nothing else to carry it in, he took the gym bag, aware that it made him conspicuous. He checked on her a last time, looped the DO NOT DISTURB card over the knob, and like that, he was suddenly, disappointingly, free.

Odds of vomiting on vacation:

   1 in 6

     She'd thought she was finished but she was far from done. After she changed into her black nightie and brushed her teeth, her bowels filled back up, and then when they were empty again and she was trying to lie still in bed, her stomach gurgled juicily, and rather than risk not making it, she went and sat on the pot a third time, bent forward, clenching a fist in effort, squeezing out a foamy gruel.

     She knew she was ruining his plans. She protested that she hadn't meant to. Wasn't her nightgown proof of her good intentions? It was just bad luck, like the bus, and yet she couldn't help but see it as a sign, her body betraying her true feelings, except, consciously at least, she'd hoped they would be tender toward each other this weekend, since it might be their last. Near the end of their rough patch, when she'd thought she'd lost him, they'd indulged in sad, often savage valedictory lovemaking, confusing yet unexpectedly right, as if, after so many years, they needed this intense physical closeness to properly say goodbye. Now she wanted to pay him the same tribute.

     She washed her hands well and ran a glass of water, took an exploratory sip and topped it off again. In her toiletry bag she unearthed a crumbling roll of Tums. She chewed two and tipped the glass back, doing her best to ignore the nauseating malty

35

taste. As soon as she swallowed them, she felt a cramp, as if the broken bits were burning her stomach. She couldn't imagine there was much left. She leaned over the sink, a hand cradling her gut, let out a sour bubble of a burp, and then, knowing it was pointless to resist, arranged the bath mat on the floor and folded herself down, the tiles cool against her skin, thinking she'd feel better once she got it all out of her.

Odds of a married couple making love
  on a given night:

   1 in 5

In the elevator, going down, he realized he was still buzzed from dinner, dully, and popped his eyes in an attempt to sober up. He needed to be careful. He believed from an ancient *Dateline NBC* that there were thieves who worked the casinos, pickpockets and teams of grifters that made off with slot players' coin buckets, sleight-of-hand artists who lay in wait by the pay-out windows. He kept the bag tucked under one arm like an old woman with her purse, and as he slowly descended, standing still in a heavy metal box being lowered by a wire, the strangeness of the moment came over him. In the bag he had eight thousand dollars he was going to change into plastic chips he would put down on a table with the rest of their savings. It was like an errand in a dream, the motivations behind his actions lost in a convoluted backstory, his fate temporarily suspended, only the dread of the present fixing him there.

Downstairs, though it was half past ten, the front desk was mobbed with an army of dark-haired women in white puffy coats and black tights, speaking what he guessed was Italian. The concierge was gone, and rather than linger about helplessly, he

crossed the lobby with purpose, headed for the closest entrance
to the casino, as if he knew where he was going.

The slot machines were ranked in rows just tall enough so he
couldn't see over them. The lighting was as dark as it had been
in the restaurant, the overheads turned low to set the mood. As
he navigated the dim maze, all around him machines blinked
and chimed like an arcade, breaking into impromptu electronic
choruses of "Camptown Races" and "La Cucaracha" and "The
Yellow Rose of Texas." In contrast to the hectic technology, the
players were mostly older women in visors and sweatshirts—a
few on scooters—tethered to the machines by stretchy cords
clipped to their fanny packs. He was surprised to find no buckets, no clinking half dollars or tokens, just plastic cards like his
room key. Instead of showers of coins, the players won credits.
They slouched in their padded swivel chairs, purses in their laps,
tapping and tapping, mesmerized. He couldn't imagine a less
rewarding way of spending his retirement, but of course to retire
one had to have a job.

The first room of slots connected to a second, larger gallery,
just as busy, angling off to the left. It was decorated in a palatial
style, white with gold trim, all Doric columns, crown moldings
and oversized chandeliers. Here the game was video poker, and
there were more men. He saw no cages along the walls, just banks
of ATMs and stations where players could replenish their cards.
He followed the orange walkway on the carpet behind several
Sikhs in turbans and a hugely fat woman in a Sidney Crosby
jersey into a bright, high-ceilinged ballroom where servers in
gold vests whisked trays of cocktails between tables crowded

with people playing craps and blackjack and a dice game he'd never heard of called Pai Gow. The cashiers were all the way in the back, making him walk the gauntlet like a hayseed with his bag under one arm.

The casino floor was like a raucous party, each table cheering and groaning over the action. A surprising number were ringed by young African couples in formal eveningwear, as if they'd just come from a wedding. There were sizable Chinese and Indian contingents, less well-dressed, and a flock of tall blondes who looked like models, tended by a security detail in ill-fitting suits. The sheer variety of people—from the homely to the freakishly glamorous—reminded him of flying through Heathrow in the eighties. These jet-setters had traveled thousands of miles to be here on a Friday night, and they weren't going to bed early. They raised their glasses to the winners, laughed at the mock-agony of the losers, then bet again. For them gambling was fun, a decadent pleasure—the same it should have been for him, since he was playing with house money, except that before he'd wagered a penny he was already a quarter million in the hole.

He wasn't a gambler. He'd never been. While walking through the pit was exciting, like being right on the sideline for a big game, he was mostly intimidated, reminded of how little experience he had. Their one time in Vegas, they'd confined themselves to the simplest games, blackjack and roulette, quitting after they'd each lost their agreed-upon stake of five hundred dollars. Craps was a complete mystery, as was baccarat. Likewise, the intricacies of the seniors' slot machines with their specials and progressive jackpots were beyond him. At this point he was the exact opposite of a gambler, interested only in what gave him the best chance to win. He'd already taken the greatest risk in his life and lost. The best he could hope for was to break even.

The few roulette wheels he passed were American—a green double zero glowed atop one pylon showing the recent winners. They also had a $5,000 limit, and so were useless to him. At each he noted how many people were playing straight black, how many red. It didn't matter, the odds were even, but he was pleased to see they were equally piled with chips, as if that made his plan more credible.

In keeping with the illusion of fiscal respectability, scrolled Beaux Arts grillwork fronted the cashiers' windows, backed by two-inch-thick plexiglas. Only a few were open. As at a bank, a short line of players, all men, waited between gold velvet ropes. He joined them, alert for anyone lurking. Above, protruding from the ceiling like spiders' eyes, a half dozen black globes kept watch, yet didn't make him feel any safer. The man in front of him dipped into his jacket and pulled out a wallet, and Art remembered the voucher for their Lucky Bucks tucked in his.

"Next in line," a woman cashier beckoned, and the man stepped forward.

"Next," another called, and Art went, setting the bag on the marble counter, glancing around casually before unzipping it.

The cashier was Emma's age, red-haired and fresh-faced, her fingers ringless. "Good evening, sir. What may I help you with?"

"I'd like to change my American dollars for chips?"

"I can help you with that. Are you a guest at the hotel?"

"I am."

"Room number?"

"Twenty-one-oh-eight." So now they would have a record. They would know they'd brought too much cash—unless they went somewhere else and traded for Canadian, easy enough.

"Thank you. And how much will you be changing with us this evening?"

He thought the amount would surprise her, but she just punched it into her computer. How often did this happen? She must have known this wasn't normal for him, with his cheap stadium giveaway bag, but she was a professional and gave no sign. He wanted to explain, but knew that would probably be worse for her. She was young and free, she didn't need to hear his middle-aged excuses.

She had him slide the stacks sideways one at a time through the brushed steel trough, laying them out, then breaking the paper seals and fitting the loose bills into a digital counter.

The readout reminded him and he grabbed for his wallet. "Plus my Lucky Bucks."

"Thank you." She printed out a slip and turned it toward him, pointing to the total. "Is that correct?"

"Yes."

He signed the slip with an old-fashioned pen on a chain, plagued by the same unease he felt when taking out a loan. Like interest, the exchange rate would kill them on both ends—if they won.

"And how would you like that, sir?"

"In thousands, please. Then a five hundred, and the rest in fifties." It sounded ridiculous, and then when she slid the chips through to him, though they added up, they seemed not nearly enough. He pushed the meager fistful deep into his pocket, plugging it with his wallet, and walked off with the empty bag, wondering at the transaction, as if she'd cheated him.

The temptation was to sit down at the nearest wheel and blow the Lucky Bucks, but because the name was a joke between them Marion would want to be there, and he made his way back through the tables, retracing his steps, except instead of taking a right into the video poker room he went straight, thinking it would take him back to the lobby faster, or at least the mall, and after passing through another dark room of slots and then a bright, deserted one of empty poker tables, certain he'd gone too far, he took the next right and found himself alone in a glass-walled solarium with a view of the Falls, along the wall beside him, incongruously, a line of potted trees strung with white Christmas lights. High-backed Adirondack benches faced the view, flanked by tall catch-all ashtrays. It was a smoking lounge, safely hidden in a cul-de-sac. The passage straight ahead led to a restaurant that had closed, the one on the right dead-ended at a service elevator. Here was the ideal place to rob someone, and naturally he'd found it.

He heard voices in the hall behind him and pictured using the bag as a weapon, flailing away at an attacker's head. The smart thing was to just give them the money, he'd always subscribed to that advice, passing it on to Emma and Jeremy, but he was too old for this bullshit, he had too little left to lose. This was his life and he would fight for it. There were at least two of them, and he could see one stabbing him, could see himself crumpling to the floor, bleeding out under the Christmas lights as the Falls silently thundered across the gorge. He thought of sitting on a bench and pretending he was just resting, but immediately vetoed the idea as stupid and cowardly. Going back was the only way out, and having no other plan, hoping to take them by surprise, he strode toward the corner, both handles gripped in his fist, ready to defend himself.

There was only one of them. In the middle of the hall, in his orange bandanna and embroidered Harley vest, hunched and talking on his cellphone, was the biker from the bus. "Baby, what do you want me to do?" he asked. "I can't be two places at once." He saw Art and nodded, pointed to the bag and gave him a thumbs-up, then turned away, covering his ear.

Feeling silly—did he think he was a secret agent?—he doubled back, finding the ballroom easily, and the video poker, though he still didn't understand how everything fit together. The layout was purposely disorienting, the honeycombed rooms skewed, connecting at odd angles, drawing the visitor deeper and deeper into the casino, in his case against his will. He'd have to get a map.

He would turn it into a joke for her, his ineptitude and panic, but first he needed to get her something for her stomach. In the lobby the Italian women were gone. The receptionist referred him to the gift shop, where a travel-sized bottle of Pepto-Bismol cost six dollars Canadian.

The elevator that finally came disgorged what appeared to be a bachelorette party wearing tiaras and drinking beer from brandy snifters. The bride-to-be, a squat blonde in a rhinestone halter top and miniskirt, was blindfolded, with a sign around her neck that read KISS ME, I'M STILL SINGLE. He was more relieved than offended when they breezed past him, laughing, but then, riding up by himself, picturing the money being lost and won downstairs, and the exotic mix of players, he felt he was missing something, as if he were leaving a party that had just started.

In the hall he swiped his key and waited for the green, shouldered the door open and locked it behind him. All the lights were on, but she was in bed, asleep. He watched her a moment as he would a child, listening, checking for any sign of breath. There, yes.

He turned off the lights, set the bag on top of the dresser and took the Pepto-Bismol into the bathroom. The toilet seat was up. On the floor lay the rumpled nest of the bath mat.

It was best to let her sleep. He went into the sitting room to turn off the lights. The panorama was just as impressive, the Falls tireless. He was glad he'd asked for the top floor. He dipped a finger in the champagne bucket—the water was tepid. He'd have to grab some ice tomorrow, try again. At their age, maybe romance was patient instead of frenzied, but just the idea made him think of Wendy urging him on, pleading with him to fuck her harder, and he turned his head as if to look away.

How much of his life did he need to forget? He was too used to going to bed unhappy with himself, vowing to do better. He hadn't expected it tonight, but here he was again, frowning in the mirror as he brushed his teeth.

Marion had taken the same side she slept on at home. He

climbed in his side, and she stirred, murmured something, then rolled over so he could spoon her. As he fitted his knees behind hers, pressing against her back, his front made contact with the slippery, satiny fabric of the nightgown he liked.

Even sick, she had worn it for him. He was at once grateful and ashamed. In an attempt to express this, he embraced her gently, resting his chin on her shoulder. He didn't mean to wake her.

"Okay," she said, "we're sleeping."

"We're sleeping," he echoed, and soon it was true, they were.

Later, in the middle of the night, she got up to use the bathroom. She felt better, but still wasn't quite right. Sitting there with her eyes closed, she could just hear, through the window by the tub, the rushing of the Falls. When she was done, she held the blind aside.

The spotlights were off. Instead of red, the Falls fell a ghostly white. The clouds were gone, and moonlight lay bright on the snow. She turned the bathroom light off and picked her way through the foreign darkness to the sitting room windows overlooking the gorge and stood there watching the Falls and the stars, sharp and twinkling in the cold, silvering her arms.

If he comes to me now, she thought. If I don't turn around but just think of him, and he comes to me.

That terrible summer she'd wished on a falling star for him to come back to her, and he had, though it hadn't made either of them happy. Maybe this wasn't any different, and yet she was ready, if he would come to her, unbidden, to try again. The longer she stood there, the more she questioned whether she truly meant it or just wanted to prove that connection between them still existed—or didn't. That was possible too, that she was looking for confirmation she was doing the right thing.

It was a childish wish, unrealistic. The cold from the window made her shiver, and after rubbing her arms to smooth her goose-bumps, she relented, turning to find the room empty, only the alien furniture attending her. She went back to bed and lay next to him, wide awake now. She recalled that summer, the stars over the lake, all of his sorry promises. She could have said no then and thrown him out, as Celia had counseled. Beside her, he slept peacefully, which she thought was wrong. When he reached for her, she fended off his hand and rolled away, punching her pillows as if he were bothering her.

Odds of the sun coming up:

    1 in 1

The next morning, as if to erase the night before, they made love. He was tentative yet pesky, rubbing against her. She was barely awake.

"Seriously?" she said, since his excitement had nothing to do with her, but gave in, sleepily hiking up her nightgown. "Try not to press too hard on my stomach."

"I won't," he promised, and then paid too much attention to honoring the request, locking his elbows so he hovered above her. The bed was less giving than their pillowtop at home, and his wrists hurt. It had been so long he was afraid he would explode, and proceeded slowly. The heat of her always astonished him, as if deep inside, like the earth, she possessed a fiery core. He was quiet, deliberate, focused on her forehead, her eyebrows, the hollows of her collarbone. She tipped her chin up, and he descended to kiss her throat.

His breath was sour and she turned her head to one side, closed her eyes as if to steal a few more minutes of sleep, murmuring with pleasure to encourage him. His lips on her neck stirred ticklish beginnings. Too soon he pulled away from her throat, but she wasn't invested enough to correct him. She peeked and found him working intently, his face slightly pained, as if he had a toothache. As he quickened, she arched, squeezing her arms against her ribs to push her breasts together, a trick that never failed. He seized, clenched, then exhaled, let his head drop.

They chastely kissed, politely traded their most solemn pledge—perilous any other time, yet exempt here, as if this space were sacred—staying together until she patted his side to let him know he could roll off.

Their room faced east, and the curtains were edged with bright sunlight.

"Looks like it's going to be a nice day," he said.

"I thought it already was," she said, and excused herself to use the bathroom.

He lay back in the pillows, dazed and emptied from his efforts, limbs splayed, contemplating the rough popcorn ceiling, his mind wiped clean. Right up until she lifted her nightgown, he hadn't been sure she would have him. After thirty years she was still inscrutable, and while normally that was frustrating, it produced in moments like this an abject gratitude, a feeling of having been rewarded spectacularly for enduring those long, brittle stretches of indifference. He was pleased enough with his performance— she'd seemed happy with it—and congratulated himself on his persistence. He was convinced there was a lesson in it. No matter what happened, all he needed to do was keep trying.

In the bathroom, cleaning herself, she knew it had been a mistake, undertaken casually, without thought of the conse- quences, as if this were any other weekend. She had to be more careful. Making love was a way of laying claim to each other, both of them openly agreeing to renew that bond. After all of their problems, she wanted foremost to be honest—her fear was that after the fact he might accuse her of premeditation—but their habits were so entrenched, and she didn't want to hurt him. She figured it would hold him till tomorrow at least.

"How's your stomach?" he asked when she returned.

"It's okay. Where's the clicker?"

"By the TV."

She grabbed it and he lifted the covers to let her back in.

Since neither of them was working, they'd developed the bad habit of sleeping late and watching TV in bed, checking the news and weather, then surfing her cooking and home makeover shows. Here she didn't feel guilty about it, and indulged herself, seeing what the Barefoot Contessa was making.

"I wonder how late the buffet serves brunch," he said.

"You're not serving me breakfast in bed?"

"We could."

"I'm just kidding."

He went to the bathroom, then paraded in front of her to open the drapes, letting in the blinding light. He stood there like a hairy cherub, admiring the view.

"People are already out there taking pictures. Hey, they've got horse-and-buggy rides."

All she wanted to do was watch her show, but no, he needed her attention. He was such a boy.

"Why don't you go take your shower?" she said.

"Want me to holler for you?"

"No, I want to see how this turns out."

Once he was gone, the bare stage of the room made her excuse all the more glaring. He was playful after they made love, frisky, yet she felt no residual giddiness, no surge of energy, only fatigue and a vague bitterness. She wasn't angry with herself so much as at her expectations—that once again she'd fooled herself into doing something she knew wouldn't help in the long run. She'd felt the same way with Karen at the end, but then she'd attributed it to guilt and the stalemate of their situation. Now there was no one she was trying to be faithful to but herself, and she couldn't even do that.

In the bathroom he was singing. She muted the TV to hear.

"Try to understand," he crooned. "Try to understand. Try try try to understand. He's a ma-gic man."

They were seeing Heart tonight, a band he mistakenly thought she'd liked when she was a teenager, because he'd liked them as a teenager. As he did the solos, ridiculously impersonating the various instruments, she lay there listening, clicker in her lap, not understanding how he could be that oblivious, and that happy, both of which, she thought, were at least partly her fault.

Odds of surviving going over the Falls in a barrel:

   1 in 3

He met Wendy through the United Way. The two of them
were volunteer chairs of their respective insurance companies'
charitable giving, and the second Wednesday of each month
drove into United Way headquarters in Cleveland for a board
meeting. Before he knew her at all, he remembered her name
that way: Wendy, Wednesday. He would have said she wasn't his
type—dark and petite, cool in her navy suits, richly lipsticked,
her hair pulled back severely. She was also married, a full carat
stone prominent on her finger, though he would have equally
had no business with her if she were single. She was younger
than he was, in her late twenties, with an MBA from Wheaton.
She carried a calculator in her briefcase and made a show of
consulting it during meetings, as if someone had nominated her
treasurer. The first time he talked to her directly was to contra-
dict her assertion that Children's Hospital received enough
money from public tax dollars, a claim she defended privately
via e-mail the next day with a breakdown of their expenses. He
retaliated that afternoon with the latest numbers from their larg-
est suburban hospital, earning him an immediate response:
Apples and oranges.

If oranges cost more, he replied, *why would we want fewer
apples?*

They chatted before the next meeting. She called him Arthur, a name he'd never liked until he heard her say it. Her hands were tiny, almost childlike, holding her coffee. A delicate silver cross rode the pulse in the hollow of her throat. She had a way of smiling wider when she disagreed with a point he was making, effectively scrambling whatever argument he was formulating. He suspected she knew her effect on him, laughing as they went over their fellow board members' pet projects. Hers was the Visiting Nurses' Association, because, she admitted, her mother was a visiting nurse.

"Still is," she said, nodding with pride. "So why are you Children's white knight?"

"I used to work there when I was young and idealistic."

"And now you work for the bad guys."

"They're not the bad guys."

"*We*," she said. "*We're* not the bad guys."

"Right. We're not the bad guys."

She laughed, rocking her head back to expose her neck. "Oh my God, you're still an idealist. How do you do it? And keep your job, I mean."

"I'm not, really."

"I don't believe you," she said.

He wasn't used to women flirting with him, married or otherwise, and convinced himself he was mistaken, but then, during the meeting, when the guy from Sohio started in with his Free Trees program, she turned to him and rolled her eyes.

They e-mailed inconsistently. He looked forward to seeing her, picturing what outfit she'd wear (the gray pinstripe was a favorite), and became accustomed, once a month, to driving the last few miles of 90 into the city sporting an insuppressible erection. When she missed a meeting because she was on vacation, he couldn't help but note how dull it was.

You missed me, she divined. *That's so sweet.*

After writing and deleting it twice, he replied: *I did.*

Because it was true, and they were both married, and it was just work—volunteer work!—nothing he took home with him. He was flattered and happy to have her as a friend, though even then that was a lie, because he'd begun to think of asking her to lunch, which was personal, and out of his way, since her office was in Lakewood, and he would never ask her to drive into the city. She would know, anyway, that he was proposing more than lunch. He was afraid of what she'd think of him because he'd already thought it himself. She was right, he was an idealist, he had no defense against his desires, only the conviction that, being sympathetic, they belonged together. He had no plan, no goal other than declaring his love for her and hoping she wouldn't laugh at him.

Fortunately she was more experienced than he was. When he finally mustered the courage to casually suggest, after one meeting, that they should have lunch sometime, she smiled widely and said, "I think you need to think about that, Arthur."

Driving home, he thought she could have just said no.

I've thought about it, he wrote the next day.

Good, she replied.

I think it's apples and oranges.

It's not, she wrote. *And that's not what I asked you to think about.*

She proposed that for a week they not talk to each other, to seriously figure out what they were doing. Because he cared for her, he tried. He ate without tasting his food, sighed in his car on the way to work. At home he was scattered, unable to follow the dumbest sitcoms. It seemed everyone in the world was making jokes.

Marion asked if he was all right. He was so quiet.

He was just tired, it had been a long day, he had a headache— the same vague excuses she'd used on him for years. He was surprised and disappointed at how easily she accepted them. He thought he must be obvious, since the feeling never left him, and then wondered how well she really knew him. He hadn't had to say a word to Wendy and she understood perfectly.

Alone, with no one to discuss it with, he was prey to his imagination. He weighed calling her office, but worried that he might frighten her. His great fear was that he would go in next month and she wouldn't be there. Finally, on the fifth day, he wrote her a carefully worded e-mail, apologizing, saying he'd resign from the board if she was uncomfortable working with him.

Who would that help? she immediately replied.

I need to see you, he wrote.

They chose an Italian place downtown and then didn't go in. It was February, the ice on the lake just breaking up. They held hands in her car as she drove to the overlook. The beach was deserted, gulls on the shuttered pavilion puffed against the wind. That was twenty years ago, and he still remembered the way she turned and looked at him before they kissed— despairing, beseeching. She'd warned him beforehand that she had a history. She needed him to be kind. He promised he would be, not seeing, in his newfound happiness, how he could ever betray her.

Odds of a couple taking a second honeymoon
  to the same destination:

  1 in 9

They ate the buffet with several hundred other guests, half of them elderly Chinese men, it seemed to Marion, all of them grim and silent, waiting in line and then processing with their trays past chafing dishes heaped with greasy, lukewarm breakfast food. The flip side of last night's restaurant, this was where the losers came to refuel. The place was set up like a giant food court, formica tables smeared with ketchup, sprinkled with salt. Art went back, fighting against the tide for a handful of napkins to swab theirs.

His plate was brimming, French toast, sausage and bacon swimming in maple syrup. All she could handle was black coffee and a plain bagel. The view, as usual, was the Falls, sharp as a postcard. The sky was cloudless, and the sun bleached the spume bright as the snow, a blinding white curtain, half a rainbow arcing from the misty tip of Goat Island down to the cold blue roil of the gorge. On the American side, dark dots swarmed the railings. She was surprised by the number of people—most of them lovers, she supposed, here to celebrate themselves.

"How is it?" he asked, pointing his fork at her coffee. She

hadn't touched her bagel, and wouldn't. She already regretted the waste.

"Awful. How's yours?"

"Remind me to order breakfast tonight."

He'd brought a stack of brochures from the lobby and shuffled through them between bites. She was fine with the horse-and-buggy ride, but the helicopter was out.

"We have to go to Ripley's."

"Do we have to?"

"Yes." He put it aside. "And definitely Madame Tussaud's."

"Didn't we see that last time?"

"It was good, as I remember."

"You remember that?"

"You don't? I'm sure it's all changed by now anyway. The House of Frankenstein?"

"Pass."

"Rock Legends Wax Museum?"

"I thought that was tonight."

"Well played. Ride Over the Falls? Mystery Maze?"

His enthusiasm wearied her, but after the twin disasters of last night and this morning, she was determined, out of fairness—if these truly were their last hours together—to be good company. At the end, she and Karen barely spoke, each of them disappointed with the other, and in Marion's case, herself. This was different. Art was reasonable to a fault, and she, as Celia liked to remind her, was too accommodating. Of all the couples they knew, she thought they had the best chance of making an amicable separation. Between the two of them they'd find a way to explain it to the children. They'd sit down and calmly lay out their plan as the best for everyone, just as they'd have to explain the bankruptcy and its residual effects. She expected tears from Emma, while Jeremy would be silently angry, as if they'd lied to him all these years instead of each other. It wouldn't be easy by any means, but other people had done it. Holidays would be awkward, with the house gone—but there, she was being silly, it was already gone, their rooms with their childhoods gathering dust, their books and toys and skates and games. They would give the children the pick of the furniture, except they were both living in apartments. It made no sense to pay for storage for things no one wanted. Art had gone over this with her months ago; only now did its full meaning sink in. She resisted it. She'd make room in her new place, even if it meant sleeping in Emma's old bed, though that might be strange when she had overnight guests—Art, for starters, since that had been the plan.

She shook her head to banish the image and took another sip of watery coffee.

"What?" Art asked.

"Nothing you want to hear."

"Try me."

"Trust me," she said. "You don't."

"I trust you."

That he could be so earnest—still—spurred her.

"I was trying to imagine what's going to happen to us."

"Good things."

"I was thinking I might take Emma's bed if she doesn't want it."

"It's not very big." Meaning he disagreed.

"I'm not going to have a lot of room."

"You'll have more than I will. I could take it."

"That makes no sense. You're too tall for it. The only bed that fits you is our bed." Which was what he wanted her to take, charging her with being the keeper of their marriage bed. She'd had the job far too long already.

"Let's cross that bridge when we come to it. If we come to it."

"I think we've come to it." She gestured to the room at large. He had no answer for her.

"I told you you didn't want to hear it."

"No, it's fine. I mean, we have to be prepared."

"Like the Boy Scouts," she said, saving him.

"That's us." He did the salute.

He pushed his tray aside and laid out the brochures in a line facing her, like tarot cards. "Okay," he said, as if the question was settled. "Not everything is open, so this is what we're looking at. I was thinking we'd do the horse-and-buggy ride first, then Journey Behind the Falls, since they're in the same place, then lunch in the Skylon Tower for the big view, then go over to Clifton Hill for the cheesy stuff. That way if we're running late we can cut that short. It's all open tomorrow."

"I was worried."

"I don't know if you're interested in the Bird Conservatory. It's like an indoor rain forest you walk through. I thought it looked interesting."

"Sure," she said with chipper conviction, to show she was game. Why did it feel like a lie?

First he had to go to the casino across the street to exchange some money, which led to the vision of him standing in the corner by the safe, stuffing the pockets of his barn coat with packets of bills like a bank robber. She waited for him in the sitting room, checking her Facebook, boasting to old high school friends that she was going to see Heart tonight. Emma had posted pictures of her and Mark from their trip to Winter Carnival in Montreal— Emma skating, Mark eating a cone of maple snow, the two of them kissing in the ice hotel. At Christmas Emma had been coy about their plans for the spring, when both of their leases were up. Marion had asked if getting a place together wouldn't make sense, given their rents, and thought Emma had been close to telling her they were. They looked happy, and rather than feel envious, Marion thought it was right. It was their time. She'd had hers.

She clicked through the pictures, occasionally glancing at the view, not minding the time alone, though after half an hour she wondered what was taking him so long. The thought that he'd been robbed was absurd, the way it made her feel sorry for him, as if he were a victim, and she squashed it. He was probably just running another errand crucial to his scheme. Despite his protestations of openness, she knew he didn't tell her everything, just as she knew they wouldn't have been there for a romantic weekend if not for the casino. As living, breathing proof, here she sat with the roses and unopened champagne while he was off somewhere chasing money.

"Sorry," he said when he came back in. The hotel next door was owned by the same resort, so he had to go to a currency exchange where the rate was so bad that he decided to find an actual bank, and then he figured while he was at it he might as well turn the money into chips, which he showed her, dipping into his pocket and opening his hand.

In his palm sat five orange chips, a purple and a black.

"How much is that?" she asked.

"Six thousand American."

"You're like Jack with his magic beans."

"Let's hope so," he said.

He put them in the safe, apologizing again. They'd only have to do it once more, tomorrow night, right before they played.

"I'm going to need you to do that," he said, as if she might refuse.

"I can't imagine it's that hard. You just walk up and ask for some chips."

"They'll make you sign for it, but it's completely legal."

"Unlike what you just did."

"That's right, I'm an international criminal."

"With a handful of magic beans."

"I also have to pee."

"I should too, before we go. How cold is it?"

"It's not bad," he said. "Maybe twenty?"

He'd thought they could take the scenic incline down to Table Rock, as they had on their honeymoon, but it was closed for the winter, and they had to retrace their steps and wait for a shuttle bus, which was so packed they gave their seats to an old Japanese couple. The driver had the heat blasting, and with nothing in her stomach, she felt clammy and feverish. It didn't help that someone smelled like a cigar. She held on to the pole, bracing her legs every time they braked.

"You okay?" he asked.

"Well," she said, "I like this bus better than the last one."

Outside, in the parking lot at the bottom of the incline, the cold spray revived her, needling her cheeks, and the Falls' monolithic roar, all around them now. As they crossed the strip of park, the noise mounted. "You can really feel it," Art said, patting his heart, and took her gloved hand in his. A clear skin of ice encased the tree branches and gas lamps and railings, the snow glazed to a shine. Only a crunchy scattering of salt kept the walkways clear.

They'd been here before, on this exact same path. Except for the weather, nothing had changed. Behind them rose the boxy seventies hotels and spiky observation towers. Ahead loomed the dour granite mock-Victorian welcome center like a museum, and the plaza overlooking the brink, teeming with drenched and happy tourists snapping away. The scene had the strange familiarity of a dream or fairy tale, as if the place had waited thirty years for them to return to learn their fate, the time in between a blink in the face of eternity.

What had she done with her life? For a moment she couldn't think of anything. Become a wife and a mother. A lover, briefly, badly. Made a home, worked, saved, traveled. All with him. For him, because of him, despite him. From the start, because she was just a girl then, she'd thought they were soul mates, that it made them special, better than the other couples they knew. She'd learned her lesson. She swore she'd never be fooled again, not by anyone, and yet she'd fought for him as if he were hers, and then, having won, didn't know what to do with him. Still didn't. That was her fault, she freely admitted it, but after all, wasn't the whole world held together by inertia?

They picked their way through the plaza, careful not to intrude on anyone's pictures, and found an open spot at the rail. When the wind kicked up, the spray billowed over them, musty as lake water. She dried her sunglasses and put them back on, their lenses improving on nature, deepening the rainbow that rose from the lip of the Falls and dropped to the gorge below. Here, hard by the rushing current, with a view of the rapids upstream, she could appreciate this wasn't just a river but a whole great lake pouring over a cliff. Feet from the edge, gulls stood on rocks as whitecaps surged past. The blue water turned a sea-green like the curl of a wave, broke and flew, foaming in overlapping sheets as it fell away, constantly, endlessly. She'd forgotten the raw force of it—the exhilarating danger the reason they were all there.

Opposite, on Goat Island, a quarter mile across the invisible border, their American compatriots waved. Sun sparkled off the relentless water. At her feet, beyond the railing, clinging to the badly patched concrete wall, rested pennies people had tossed for luck. A paper cup slalomed between the rocks like a toy boat, dipped out of sight at the last second, then rose, flipped into the air as if thrown and went over. How soothing it must be to the suicidal, she thought, knowing all you had to do was jump the railing. But you still had to jump. People came from all over the world to do it. She wondered how many had stood right here, unable to take that last step.

He squeezed her hand. "Don't move," he said, and vanished into the crowd.

She was surprised at the number of Indian families, the women's saris flowing below their winter coats. The men circled, concentrating like cinematographers on their video cameras, intent on capturing every moment. She remembered Art doing the same thing at Gettysburg or SeaWorld, and missed the children, if not those strained and shrill years. From bitter experience, Celia had told her not to stay for their sake, and while Marion believed she hadn't, if she and Art had accomplished nothing else, she was grateful they'd been able to provide them with a stable home.

As she reflected on what this meant now that they were breaking up the house, he returned holding a red rose in a cellophane cone like the street vendors sold at stoplights. She thought of tossing it over the railing and immediately disowned the gesture as mad. He was sweet, he was devoted to her. Wasn't that enough?

"You know we already have roses."

"I can take it back."

"Yeah, just try."

He took a shot of her sniffing it, prompting a German woman to offer to shoot them together. He hugged her from behind, his arms crossed over hers as if to keep her warm. When he kissed her neck, a drop of water snuck under her collar, making her squirm.

"Sorry."

"That's all right, I'm already soaked. Where's this horse-and-buggy ride you keep promising? And more important, is it dry?"

It was the wrong weekend for a carriage ride. The line snaked halfway around the welcome center. She didn't think she could make it without something to eat, so they compromised, wandering the food gallery on the ground floor until they found a sushi place for a fortifying bowl of udon noodles, the Japanese equivalent of grandma's chicken soup. The windows were steamed, and the hot broth made her want to stay there and people-watch, but he was determined to romance her.

There were only five carriages. For more than an hour they waited in the cold as the line shuffled by the great floral clock, its blooms browned and iced over, its hands stilled for the winter. They huddled for warmth, groaned with everyone else when the wind pushed the spray their way. A number of the couples were newlyweds, including a bridal party that must have had a reservation, because they went directly to the head of the line, their own photographer taking shots of the bride and groom in a gilded white carriage with the Falls and its ever-present rainbow behind them, first alone, then attended by their bridesmaids and groomsmen, with their respective families, and finally all together. It took a while, the other carriages loading and unloading to one side as the photographer and the bride's mother fussed with the bride's dress. Marion watched the lucky couple leaning in and whispering, laughing and touching, kissing for the camera. How young they were, how new. Today they were celebrities, set apart like royalty. She remembered the feeling and felt sorry for them, knowing it wouldn't last, and yet, when they left without taking a ride, waving to everyone, she applauded along with the rest of the line, wishing them luck. Impossibly, she wanted to go back and start over, as if, this time, they might find a way not to ruin things.

She hoped she and Art would get the same carriage, and thought it was a sign when they did, though he didn't seem to notice. The horse was a fat dapple gray with a floppy red bow on her tail that didn't quite hide the poop bag. The blankets were still warm from the last couple. They snuggled under them, holding hands as the driver recited his monologue in what she first suspected was a put-on Irish brogue but soon conceded was the real thing.

He told them about the ice bridge that formed below the American Falls in cold years. They could see it down there on their right. In the old days, workmen from the Grand Hotel shoveled it so visitors could walk across for a close-up view. There was a restaurant that set up shop on the bridge, it was that solid, till 1912, when a freak thaw washed away a pair of young sweethearts and another fellow, and that was the end of that. Though, sure, if you looked down there right now with a pair of spyglasses, you could bet you'd see footprints.

"That's wild," Art said.

"That's the least of it," the driver said. "There's stories to fill a book, if folks have the stomach for 'em."

This was his shtick, the dark raconteur. For the rest of the ride he entertained them with tales of doomed daredevils and failed rescues and gaslit murders. As one misfortune succeeded another, Art looked to her and shrugged, as if to say he hadn't meant to encourage him. She had to laugh. Nothing ever turned out the way he wanted. She patted his hand to show it was all right and pointed at the gulls flying far below in the gorge, tiny white crosses sailing over the swirling rapids. Away from the Falls there was no spray, no crowd. They were traveling at a walking pace, the unhurried clip-clop of hooves and the driver's rich lilt lulling her. She closed her eyes and felt the sun on her face, sat there basking, leaning against Art, and for the first time since they'd arrived she was glad they came. There was a peace in giving up, if only momentarily, and she was sorry when the ride was over. For their picture, she held her rose straight upright between them, and, like a bride, tipped her chin, closed her eyes and gave him a perfectly innocent kiss.

Odds of a U.S. citizen filing for bankruptcy:

1 in 17

As everywhere else, there was a good-sized line for Journey Behind the Falls. It was past lunchtime, but it made no sense to go back up the hill, so again they waited, milling in an overheated anteroom cordoned with yellow nylon rope and abuzz with a dozen languages. There was no off-season here, the Falls were always on. Art didn't know why he thought the place would be all theirs, and wanted to apologize. He had the ring in his pocket. Having just missed an opportunity, he was hungry for another.

In so many ways, they were here because of his wishfulness. As a child, even as a teenager, he was a dreamer, insulated from the larger world by school and his parents' house, the limits of their comfortable suburb. He was a straight-A student, used to acing tests with minimal effort. It was only in his senior year that he realized life might not be as easy as he'd thought. He was co-captain of the math team. His fellow co-captain, Boaz Parmalee, a transfer from Israel who would later help develop the first iteration of Windows, began the season with a perfect tournament, then the next month repeated the feat, landing him on the cover of the school paper. Competing against the best in the county, Art had been content to place in the top ten. Now he crammed for each tournament, staying up late in his gloomy attic room, running through proofs, overloading his brain. His scores improved, though he still trailed Boaz, yet every time he sat down to face the blank test booklet, he believed this time might be different, and was surprised when the results confirmed that once again he'd lost. The team won the county easily and placed third in states, the school's best showing ever, but while Art smiled with Boaz as they each held a jug handle of the trophy, he was thinking—and part of him was still convinced—if he'd just studied harder, he could have beaten him.

Now, well into middle age, he'd changed shockingly little. If, as he liked to think, his greatest strength was a patient, indomitable hope, his one great shortcoming was a refusal to accept and therefore have any shot at changing his fate, even when the inevitable was clear to him. He knew the house was out of their range when she first e-mailed him the listing. He only went along to the showing to make her happy, and then, after seeing the high ceilings and tile fireplaces, she wanted it. It was a bargain, she insisted, drawing his attention to the woodwork and the leaded glass, the actual plaster walls. The strength of her desire surprised him. He wanted to fulfill it, as if, out of gratitude, she might transfer that ardor to him.

Technically they shouldn't have qualified for the mortgage, even with both of them working. The down payment mostly came from the money his mother had left him from the sale of the family manse in Shaker Heights, a guilty windfall he thought would help pay for the childrens' college, not that far off. With the stroke of a pen their nest egg was gone, and they were the owners of a leaky old showplace that still had the original knob-and-tube wiring from the twenties. The furnace was a massive octopus swaddled in a full-body cast of asbestos, the plumbing an illegal mix of steel, PVC and lead. They couldn't afford to do everything at once, and believed the realtor's inspector when he said the roof would last a few more winters. The first major storm, melt from heavy ice dams stained the second-floor ceilings, spreading sepia blooms that grew daily, the steady dripping a torture, until a roofer who advertised emergency repairs could fit them into his schedule. That spring they cashed in a mutual fund to redo the roof, screwing up their taxes. Every year it seemed there was another project, while the principal on their mortgage barely lessened, thanks to the ballooning escrow. They redid the bathrooms, painted the exterior trim a different color, waterproofed the basement. When he was seeing Wendy, they were repointing the chimneys. Whenever he thought they were finished, Marion had another idea. From the beginning she'd wanted to gut the cramped fifties-era kitchen, and when Jeremy graduated from college, relieving them, finally, of the burden of tuition, interest rates were so low that he gave in and they took out a home equity loan that amounted to a second mortgage.

He knew better than to try to live on credit, especially at his age, but money was cheap. The interest rate was nothing compared to the penalty they'd pay for breaking into their IRAs early. The money was there—and more, thanks to his firm's generous stock option—they just couldn't touch it. It was a simple liquidity problem that time would naturally fix. Until then, the loan would bridge the gap. This way they'd get to enjoy the kitchen, and what better place to invest than their own home?

The renovation took longer and cost more than they budgeted for, but Marion was happy with her new custom cabinets and six-burner cooktop and double wall ovens, and when they entertained friends, they were sure they'd made the right choice. Then, as part of a supposed restructuring, the nursing home reduced her hours. A few months later the parent company, HealthSouth, closed the facility and cut loose the remaining staff.

The mistake, he thought later, was assuming the world would go along from day to day the way they did. From thirty years in insurance, he knew it was impossible to see the future. You hedged your bets by minimizing risk, denying coverage to anything remotely borderline. In retrospect, the chances places like AIG and Countrywide were taking were insane, though, under normal circumstances, as with their own debts, they would have never been asked to make good on them all at once.

The crash was too fast, or he was too slow. Like his mother, he prided himself on being a buy-and-hold investor, and expected a rebound, if only the vaunted dead-cat bounce. Their portfolio was conservative and diversified, but by the time he made up his mind to pull their money out, the Dow was below 8,000 and everything had slid. Though Ohio Life wasn't involved in default swaps, it was an equity company, and the common stock that made up the foundation of his retirement was now trading south of a dollar. In the shakeout the firm was easy prey for an Asian investment group, who merged it with Northeast Direct, a former competitor, and changed the name to Heartland Financial. The layoffs started immediately, officially called a reduction in team size. At orientation the new CFO confirmed there could be more. Employees would also be responsible for their own retirement and health insurance plans. As a corporation and as individuals, they had to be realistic. He didn't need to remind them, they were dealing with a whole new economy.

He'd been there nearly twenty years, and relied on his seniority to protect him. It seemed to, through the early rounds of cuts. The new head of Human Resources—a hired gun from Chicago— had come for friends on both sides of his office, a brawny security guard trailing behind like a bouncer with a copy-paper box. The drill was simple: hand over your badge and take your personal possessions. No farewell lunch, no sheet cake, no gag gifts. The day was always Friday, as if, over the weekend, they might forget their lost colleagues. The practical result was that the survivors resented and feared management, and now had to do the work of two or three people, meaning they were always playing catch-up.

He made it to July. Normally he'd have been at Pymatuning, enjoying the cool of the lake. To showcase his industriousness, he'd skipped vacation, a tactic Marion disliked but agreed was probably smart.

They came for him in the morning, before coffee break. He'd been expecting them but was still panicked, a subtle vertigo taking hold. As he rooted through his desk, salvaging old address books and dried-up pens and *It's a Girl!* cigars, his skin flushed. Though the office was over-air-conditioned, his forehead was sweating. He wanted to say he wasn't ready, except they didn't care. As a precaution he'd updated his resumé, but, typically, hadn't sent it anywhere. He was a hard worker, a self-starter, a team player. In the end he was a victim of his own diligence. His accounts were perfect, all ready for someone else to take over.

In his entire life he'd never been fired. Even as the guard walked him out to the parking lot to make sure he left the campus, Art couldn't believe it was happening. He set the box with Marion's and the children's pictures on the passenger seat, buckled in and pulled out, passing the security shack like he had thousands of times before, only this time he wasn't coming back.

He wanted to be calm for Marion. As he drove, he ran through what he could say to her, none of it comforting. He was fifty-two, too old to start over. He'd missed break, and stopped for a coffee at his regular Dunkin' Donuts, doing the drive-thru. As he waited at the window, he watched the staff inside working the counter in their visors and uniforms and thought he was no longer part of that world. He paid, fitted the cup in the cup holder and rejoined traffic. With his windows up and the air-conditioning on, he floated down the commercial strip in motorized silence, separated from the bright, bustling life outside as if it were a film projected all around him, his own personal IMAX experience that would have to end and release him, except it didn't, it went on and on, street after street, light after light, until he was only a couple blocks from home. He considered stopping at a bar, if he could find one that was open. He could drive down to the lake and walk along the beach, but the idea recalled Wendy and he nipped it. There was really nowhere else to go, just as there was nothing to say besides the flat fact that he'd been fired. And then, when he pulled into their driveway and thumbed the button, the garage door rolled up to show both bays were empty.

He needn't have worried. She was understanding, having recently been let go herself. It was harder telling the children, a job he partly ceded to her, accepting their condolences from the kitchen extension. A trickier question was who else they should tell. There was no way of stopping her from sharing the news with Celia, but he didn't want their friends to know, which she didn't quite follow, since they were all aware of her situation. In deference to his pride she honored his request, keeping his secret even after Mrs. Khalifa deduced the truth.

It was obvious. He was around the house all week, running errands and working in the yard when he wasn't online applying for any job within a hundred miles. He was overqualified for most of the positions, or so he told himself when they never got back to him. Mornings he sat at the granite-topped island in the kitchen with his coffee, poring over the sparse want ads in the *Plain Dealer*. Despite thirty years managing corporate accounts, he wasn't a CPA. He'd always considered himself capable, but what skills did he really have? He couldn't weld, he didn't have his Class B driver's license. Maintenance people were needed for apartment buildings in the city. *Applicant will be responsible for basic plumbing repairs.* There, he couldn't even be a janitor.

The hardest part was wondering what he could have done differently. With no recourse and so much time to himself, he mulled over the past like a blown putt, but couldn't isolate one crucial misstep. It was his whole life, the sum total of his short-comings, that had brought him here. He could blame the company and the banks for being greedy and overextending themselves, putting the country at risk and then socking away the TARP money, and in his most constipated inner rages did, but, like his time with Wendy, the scale of his latest failure seemed an indictment of him, the timid underachiever, and he was glad his mother wasn't alive to see it.

She'd spent the last decade of her life alone, on a fixed income, fretting over every penny, reminding him so often that several times he offered to help, only to discover, as her executor, that between distributions from annuities and dividends she was making twice what he and Marion were taking home. Now, faced with dwindling resources and a constant assault of bills, he resorted to stopgap measures she would have disapproved of, paying bills late, or paying with credit cards, then paying just the minimum on the cards so each month their balance rose. Every day he dreaded the mail. Some bills had to be paid promptly—the mortgages, their health and home and auto insurance. The gas and electric had more slack, the water and sewer, the garbage pick-up, the bundled cable, internet and phone. Even when they didn't spend anything, the money was draining away. After a life dedicated to making the numbers come out right, he felt he was betraying himself.

Marion's view was that it was just money and not a true barometer of their personal worth, which was healthy but not helpful. While she did most of their discretionary spending, the checkbook was solely his province. Before heading out to the supermarket, she asked how he wanted her to pay. Beyond that, she didn't want to know how bad things were, a luxury he couldn't afford and which he naturally resented. When he tried to discuss it with her, they invariably ended up fighting over the kitchen. "Then take it back," she said. "Rip it all out and take it back, I don't care anymore." He was a reasonable man, he had no defense against her anger or her tears. His goal wasn't to make her as unhappy as he was, and so, for the sake of peace, he broke off and carried on with his crooked bookkeeping as if the problem were his alone.

Odds of surviving going over the Falls
without a barrel:

1 in 1,500,000

The sign by the ticket window said that due to weather conditions the lower observation deck was closed.

"What do you think?" Art asked, though they both knew he wanted to. Why pretend her vote was the tiebreaker? It wasn't just politeness, Marion thought. He needed her to be as excited as he was.

"We've waited this long," she said.

While they were still dry, they had their picture taken in front of a false backdrop of the Falls in summer, the green islands inviting. She tried to smile, but was tired, and the shot on the monitor captured a put-upon hardness around her mouth.

"That's worth at least thirty dollars," he said.

"Look who's talking, Mr. Blinky."

"The other one's better anyway."

They moved on, receiving a translucent yellow poncho the thickness of a trash bag, then waiting in a cramped hallway for the elevator. She was too hot, and had Art hold her rose while she pulled off her jacket. Her back hurt from standing. Inwardly she cursed whoever came up with this crazy layout. She was trying to be supportive but could feel her patience waning. There were so many things she could be getting done at home.

Machinery whirred and whined inside the walls. A settling clank, and finally the doors rolled open, releasing a cold breeze and a line of tourists wearing the same ponchos. None of them looked wet and none of them was smiling.

"Step right in," the operator said.

Marion expected a deep freight elevator capable of taking several dozen adults, but it was average-sized, no bigger than those at the hotel. The operator squeezed in as many people as she could before closing the doors, making Marion worry about its maximum occupancy.

"Welcome to Journey Behind the Falls," the operator recited, uninterested. "The shaft we're traveling in descends a hundred and twenty feet through solid rock. It took one hundred skilled workmen three years to complete, at a cost of over one million dollars. Since then, more than forty million visitors have stood where you're standing, including Princess Diana, President Kennedy and Marilyn Monroe. As you exit, you'll see signs directing you to the two viewing portals on your right and the observation deck on the left. Please watch your step, as the tunnel floors can be slippery when wet."

Her spiel was timed to keep them occupied until the elevator reached the bottom. The first thing they saw when the doors rolled open was the line to return to the surface—twice the length of the one upstairs.

The air was dank and frigid, and the dimly lit tunnel echoed with footsteps. The walls were whitewashed, the ceiling low and rounded, the lights caged. It reminded her of the antiquated tube stations of London, designed for not just smaller crowds but, seemingly, smaller people. There was no guide, only tourists like themselves wandering around in the dark. With their hoods on, their faces shadowed, they looked like monks filing through the catacombs.

She let Art lead. They followed a sign to the Cataract Portal, cached in a dungeonlike dead end. Where the window was supposed to look out onto the Falls, the opening was plugged with ice, a blob of frozen marshmallow oozing into the room.

On the other side of a low fence meant to stop them from getting too close sat a massive black metal and glass contraption wired to a conduit on the wall.

"Must be one of the lights that makes the colors," he said.

"Not tonight it won't," she said.

"It's weird. You'd think they'd have some kind of deicing system to keep them clear."

"You're thinking like an American. It's Canada—they like ice."

The Great Falls Portal was the same, a solid block. She couldn't stifle her laughter in time. It was like paying to look inside someone's freezer.

He wasn't amused.

"I'm sorry, I think it's funny."

"I think it's a rip-off," he said, as if it were personal.

"Come on, don't be like that."

"How long did we stand in line? They should have told us.

We could have done something else instead of waiting an hour to see nothing."

Here was the brittle, rigid Art that emerged more frequently since he'd been laid off, always lurking just beneath the cheerful veneer. His mother had been the same way, affecting a patrician calm, then breaking into self-righteous tirades when the smallest thing went wrong—tipped juice boxes or overcooked steaks. They shared a sense of entitlement and a selective paranoia, as if the world were conspiring against them. Marion was hurt and angry too, but knew the world wasn't to blame. They'd had their share of good luck, more than most couples, especially after the mistakes they'd made. She didn't hold hers above his or vice versa. Like the world, no one was perfect. Forget Wendy Daigle, forget Karen. If Marion was disappointed in anyone it was herself. She'd promised not to give up on him, but at moments like this she was convinced she'd be happier alone, and felt selfish.

"Do you want to leave?" she asked. "Should we not bother with the observation deck?"

"It's closed, supposedly."

"There's got to be something open down here."

"You'd think so, but you'd think a portal would actually let you look at something too."

"I hate it when you get like this," she said, and turned away.

"I'm not 'like this'—this is like this. I don't know why you're mad at me."

The walls added a hollow echo to his words. People were coming, and they broke off, as if they could continue this later.

The tunnel was so narrow that groups had to pass in and out single file. She followed behind him, walking with the rose down at her side like a riding crop. She knew exactly why she was mad at him—because he was being petty and cynical, making her defend the stupid tourist trap he'd chosen and that she had no interest in in the first place; because he'd goaded her into doing exactly what she didn't want to do, which was fight with him; because he was acting childish, making her take on the mother's role—but as happened so often after a flare-up, once she stepped free of the arena and had a minute to reflect, she felt chastened, instantly regretful, as if she'd forgotten that keeping the peace between them was her job. Years of refereeing the children's disputes, and then her patients' and her staff's, had left her incapable of steamrolling an opponent, no matter how deserving. If she couldn't extend that fairhandedness to her husband, what kind of person was she? He was entitled to his disappointment. Besides her, it was all he had. He wasn't good on his own, and she worried that once she was gone, it might swallow him.

The line for the elevator had grown.

"Is it worth checking out the observation deck?" she asked a woman near the end.

"I guess," she said. "It's not worth sixteen dollars."

"Can you see the Falls?"

"It's crowded but you can see them."

"Thank you," Marion said.

On the way they discovered a plaque on the wall with a light right above it. MIRACLE AT NIAGARA, the header read. The picture below showed a half-naked boy sprawled on a life ring being hauled onboard the *Maid of the Mist*. In July of 1960 seven-year-old Roger Woodward and his seventeen-year-old sister had gone for a boat ride with a neighbor on the upper Niagara River. The motor flooded and the boat capsized in the rapids. While onlookers watched, the current swept the three toward Horse-shoe Falls. The sister swam for Terrapin Point and was rescued by two men from New Jersey. The neighbor went over the Falls and was killed. Roger, wearing only a bathing suit and a life jacket, suffered just a mild concussion. To this day Roger Wood-ward was still the only person not in a barrel to survive a plunge over the falls.

"I thought it was going to be about us," Art said.

"Not everything can be about us," Marion said. "Thank God."

As they went along the hall, the other plaques commemorat-ing Nikola Tesla and President Truman and Niagara's status as a honeymoon venue were less interesting, yet, as if it were a con-dition of their truce, they dutifully stopped at each one to poke fun at the canned, shallow history. Like the fake backdrop upstairs and the elevator operator's spiel, the plaques were a way to decorate the empty space they had to cross—a welcome dis-traction, since by then they'd run out of small talk.

TO OBSERVATION DECK, a sign with a helpful arrow prompted, though there was nowhere else to go. They were getting close. Traffic was passing them, purposeful families bent on seeing everything in a single day. As if swept up in their excitement, they fell in behind them. After several blind turns, they entered a tunnel filled with piercing outside light and the thrashing of falling water. Ahead, bunched at the end, silhouetted by the glare, their fellow tourists mingled like faceless shades.

They emerged squinting into the world. To the right, the Falls dropped frothing from directly above, shedding waves of spray which caked the cliff face with built-up ice the glacial blue of windshield wiper fluid and fringed the opening with gnarled, waxy stalactites. The rainbow, like the sky, seemed bigger here, brighter, right on top of them. Once the clump in front had taken their fill of pictures, she and Art squeezed up to the railing that prevented them from going down a short flight of iced-over stairs.

The observation deck proper lay below, a circle the size of a helipad ringed by snowcapped posts like tuffets. It jutted invitingly toward the gorge, overlooking the old powerhouse, its long roof a perfect slab of white. In the summer the view would be spectacular, she thought, that much closer to the edge, but this was interesting too. Downstream, though there were no footprints on it, as their driver had suggested, the ice bridge stretched to the American side, the capsized floes piled high in the middle like freshly calved icebergs, dotted with gulls. Beyond the scrim of mist that hid the base of the Falls, only a green, rushing strip of river showed, quickly disappearing under the lip of the bridge. She remembered the cup she'd seen at the top going over and pictured herself trapped like an air bubble beneath the ice, sealed off, an old childhood nightmare contracted from a bad movie, laughable, especially now, when she was trying to sort out her real fears. Celia, in her own jaded way, was right. She was the only person who could hurt herself, just as she was the only one who could help herself. Daydreaming did nothing.

Beside her, Art snapped away, all of his bitching forgotten. That he could be so easily placated confounded her. Suddenly they were supposed to be having fun.

"Good thing we didn't go back up," she said.

"Thank you." Softly spoken, it was an apology, as if he were ashamed of losing his patience. "I still don't know why they gave us ponchos."

"Maybe if it's windy. You'd definitely need them in the summer."

"It might actually be worth it then."

"It would be, with the portals. Without them, I'll go ten, no more."

"I'll say twelve."

"I think you're being generous. Did you get enough pictures?"

"More than enough."

They drank in a last look and shouldered their way through the crowd and into the darkness again. On the way back they passed people taking shots of the plaques.

The line was even longer. She didn't recall the operator mentioning any restrooms, and tried to put the idea out of her mind, just as she tried not to think of tonight's dry run, or tomorrow, or the long ride home. She imagined the boy, Roger Woodward, struggling to swim against the current. She thought she knew the dread and panic of being swept inexorably toward the edge, except that sometime in these past few months, whether to preserve her strength or her sanity, she'd stopped fighting. Now she was just floating, waiting to go over. What happened after that was beyond her control. Unlike Art, she didn't expect to be rescued.

Odds of a marriage proposal being accepted:

1 in 1.001

    The sideshow delights of Clifton Hill would have to wait. By the time they rode the glass elevator up the stalk of the Skylon Tower, the sun was setting. The gorge lay in blue shadow, the escarpment stretching to the west a shimmering gold. Their camera wouldn't capture its lambent brilliance or the sheer scale, but he took a couple of shots anyway. Below, as with the flick of a switch, the string of lights that defined the parkway came on. Traffic was stopped on the Rainbow Bridge, everyone trying to get home, the buses stuck at customs.

    He'd planned on them enjoying a leisurely lunch in the revolving restaurant as they had as newlyweds, but it was almost five. They only had time for a quick drink. At the hostess stand, Marion handed him her rose and asked him to order her a glass of Chardonnay, leaving him to secure a window table. The few available faced north, away from the Falls. The room took an hour to do a complete revolution. He chose the table that would come around the soonest, hoping there'd be some sunset left.

    He saved her the chair that would have the best view. Once he was settled, a waitress materialized at his side, as if she'd been watching him. He ordered and looked out over the neon theme park architecture of Clifton Hill and the snowy grid of the city, in the distance the dark expanse of Lake Ontario. The motion of the room was subtly disorienting, the windowsill inching past, as though he were standing still. To the east, night was already falling, and he felt a twinge of urgency.

All day he'd been carrying the box in his pocket, alert for the perfect moment. Now he pulled it out, opening it below the tabletop like a cellphone. He could place it beside her rose so she'd find it when she returned, but thought that too passive. He needed to give it to her, to formally ask her to be his again. If he was too sudden, the element of surprise might work against him, especially after what happened in the tunnels. He didn't want her to feel ambushed. She'd say the ring was too much, that they couldn't afford it—objections more practical than emotional, as if their life now was just about money, or the lack of it.

The first time he'd asked her he was making two hundred a week working for a nonprofit and living in a roach-infested studio over a TV repair shop in Slavic Village. They'd been dating nearly a year, but she had a nice apartment in University Circle with her old college roommates, trust fund babies who called in sick to their temp jobs, cruised the clubs for older men, and considered him boring and unworthy of her, the best-looking of the three. He wanted to ask her to move in with him to show her he was serious and get her away from them. He knew what she made, and studied the classifieds, canvassing real estate agencies in neighborhoods he judged safe—all without consulting her.

To make his case, he chose Shanghai Garden, a Friday night

staple, where they could eat for less than twenty dollars and take home a doggie bag with tomorrow's lunch. They sat in the back, where an oversized angelfish roamed an otherwise empty tank like a lonely ghost. He waited till they'd finished to ask her.

"What do you mean you've been looking?" she asked. "Like actually looking at apartments?"

"Not actually looking looking, just trying to see how much it would be."

"Wait wait wait wait wait," she said, holding up both hands. "You. Are out looking. For an apartment. For us."

Instead of discussing the happy possibility of spending their days and nights together, they fought. He thought he was being thoughtful and responsible. She thought he'd taken her answer for granted. Why didn't he just talk to her instead of sneaking around behind her back? Didn't he think she should have a say in her own life? He had no defense save for his good intentions, which now seemed self-serving or, at best, mistaken. One of her capping arguments was that her parents would expect them to get married. The way she said it made it sound like it might never happen and she didn't want to give them a false impression.

"Do you want to get married?" he asked.

"Come on, Art," she said, as if he were making an unfunny joke.

"Do you?"

"Stop. Nobody's marrying anybody. Jesus."

From then on, whenever he was tempted to think of a future with her, he would remember how absurd she made it seem, so that even after they'd moved in together he sometimes still felt as if he were her second choice, their situation temporary. When they finally decided to get married, it was more of a negotiation than a proposal, concerned primarily with timing, since Celia was getting remarried and didn't want to hold off making arrangements for a whole year.

Their waitress reappeared with their drinks, and he wondered where Marion was. Their dinner reservations were at six. He'd ordered a Molson draft, the same thing he had their first time. He sipped it, trying not to get too far ahead of her. The room had rotated so he could just see the Canadian end of the Rainbow Bridge. They might catch part of the American Falls but not the sunset.

She came up from behind, surprising him.

"Sorry. There was a line. I almost wet my pants. Then when I came out, you'd moved and I couldn't find you. How are we on time?"

"We're okay."

"There was this woman in there with her little girl, I swear she's one of the ones from Heart. She had the eighties rock star hair and everything."

"Which one? The blonde one or the dark one?"

"The skinny one."

"Nancy Wilson."

"Whoever. Her daughter was not having a happy time."

"You know who she's married to."

"No, enlighten me."

"Cameron Crowe."

"Help me out."

"The director. *Say Anything? Jerry Maguire?*"

"Don't turn around," she said, her eyes tracking someone behind him.

She might have been right. The woman who passed at his elbow with her daughter in hand did look like Nancy Wilson—willowy, with long teased hair and a tiny waist—though it was hard to tell from the back. She had on a black leather jacket, cigarette-leg jeans and biker boots. She was probably just a fan dressed for the concert. He couldn't imagine Nancy Wilson, with all the money in the world, eating at a place like this a couple hours before showtime, just as he couldn't imagine Nancy Wilson with a sulky four- or five-year-old daughter.

"She's got to be our age," he said. "Or older."

"All I know is, someone wants their activity book."

"Aha."

A few tables away, the woman turned to help her daughter into her booster seat, giving him a better view.

All he had to see were her eyes. Her face was leonine, iconic, calling up album covers and magazine spreads.

"Oh my God," he said, whispering, as if it were a secret. "It is her."

"Are you sure?"

"I'm sure."

Weirdly, she hadn't changed. Despite the dated hairstyle, she was still striking—high cheeks, the straight nose and full lips, the dimpled chin. Under the leather jacket she wore a frilly ver-million blouse she might have worn onstage. There was a younger woman with them, black-haired, possibly a nanny, because she was helping the girl with her napkin.

Marion sat up, obstructing his view. "Don't stare."

"I can't help it."

"She has on a ton of makeup."

"You'd think they'd have a sound check to do, or something."

"I thought you liked them smaller," she said, an allusion he could either refute or let pass. The worst thing he could do was hesitate. "And younger."

"I like *you*."

"You've got to be quicker than that."

"I do like you. And love you."

"I don't see why."

The box was a lump in his pocket. Of all the possible moments, right then he should have been able to give her a life-time of reasons, except that he felt attacked. Unfairly, he would have said, though, knowing how often he thought of Wendy—pointlessly, since it had been twenty years and in the end he'd been relieved to be free of her—he was even more skeptical of himself. He knew what he'd done. She didn't have to keep reminding him.

"I know why," he said.

"Tell me."

"Because you care about everyone, you want everything to be fair, and you'll fight for what's right."

"Did you just come up with that?"

"I did."

"I'm impressed." She raised her glass and dipped her head in tribute. "I don't think that's entirely true, but I'm impressed."

"What's not true?"

"I'm not nearly as nice as you think I am."

"You actually helped people. I didn't."

"You did what you could," she said.

"I should have never taken the job."

"It put the kids through school."

"We could have done it some other way."

To confess these misgivings secretly thrilled him, and the fact that, after everything, she would defend him. At home they would have never picked apart their lives so clinically, airing their regrets as if they were some other couple's. Like middle age, vacation provided a necessary distance, an extra perspective.

Outside it was night, blackness filling the gaps, flattening the world below to patterns of lights, a schematic view usually glimpsed from an airliner in its final descent. The room had rotated so the Rainbow Bridge was almost beside them, still packed with traffic. He thought of the house, locked and dark, the realtor's sign a public admission in the yard, and wondered if the trip had been a mistake, the plan, everything. They could ride it out another six months if they had to.

"Melody hasn't called," he asked.

"I think I've given up on Melody," she said, but dug out her phone.

"Not that it matters."

"No, nothing."

"I never thought we'd lose money on that house."

"It was a good house," she said. "It was the right house for us then. Oop—I can see the Falls. Look at the hearts."

He twisted his neck. Projected pinkly onto the curtain of falling water was a plump pair of hearts skewered by Cupid's arrow. "Very nice. The thing I worry about is the kids not having a place to come back to."

"I think they're okay with it. When was the last time they were back?"

"I still miss my old house."

"I know you do," she said.

"It would be nice to have a place for the grandchildren."

"I think that's down the road a ways, Grandpa."

"Not that far, at least for Emma. I know Mark wants kids."

"Okay, now I feel old."

The waitress appeared, pointing back and forth between their glasses. "Another round?"

Marion looked to him, the official timekeeper. If they left now they'd have just enough time to get back and change for dinner, but he was pleasantly buzzed from the beer, and the way they were talking seemed more important than making their reservation. They could see the Falls, Nancy Wilson was sitting three tables away, and rather than cut short the moment, he veered from his plan and gave the waitress the okay.

Looking back, he would see this decision as the one that determined the rest of the evening, if not the weekend, an obvious tipping point, as if by taking the first step off the path he was knowingly leading them deeper into the woods. Whether that was true or not—and they would fight over it—later he would blame himself, thinking he'd been greedy, but at the time, honestly, all he wanted to do was go on talking with her.

Odds of a 53-year-old woman being a grandmother:

1 in 3

They had an expensive bottle of Cabernet with dinner, and Irish coffees with dessert, and were tipsy enough that they took a cab the few blocks back to the hotel rather than risk slipping and falling on the icy sidewalk. She had to concentrate to make sense; her eyes stung from the effort. Through her window she could see the stars spread across the sky like a connect-the-dots puzzle and wondered what secret message they were trying to send her. She was hot in her coat, and struggled to free her arms as if it were a straitjacket. With his help she finally succeeded, smacking him in the lip with her ring. She laughed, then apologized, laid a hand on his jaw and kissed him to make it all better, when suddenly they were there, under the portico, the white-gloved valet opening the door for her, helping her out, telling her to watch her step.

The escalator made her sway, and she took Art's arm. It was bright inside, the lobby achime with the ringing of slot machines, and she was relieved when the elevator doors closed, shutting it out. She leaned against the back wall, felt the rushing uplift in her legs.

"Are you gonna make it?" he asked.

"I'm good," she said, Emma's favorite phrase, and pictured her alone in her cozy apartment in Boston, the quiet, solitary life

Marion sometimes envied, except from her Facebook page she knew Mark was taking her out for dinner and dancing. That was better anyway, Marion thought. When she was single, she and her friends used to go clubbing every weekend, coming home at daybreak with a half dozen stamps on their hands. When was the last time she really let loose? She was tired of moping around the house, waiting for the next bad thing to happen. Maybe Art had the right idea—why pretend anymore? If they were going down, they might as well do it in style.

They barely had time to use the bathroom and change. As always, the mirror reminded her that she wasn't young anymore. She hadn't been to an actual rock concert in over a decade. Lacking anything sexier, she'd brought her best dinner party outfit, a slimming pair of black slacks and a flashy silver top, but after seeing Nancy Wilson she felt self-conscious and grandmotherly.

"I hate what I'm wearing," she said, "but I don't have anything else. Sorry, what you see is what you get."

"You look fine." All he'd changed was his shirt, from a white oxford to a cornflower blue. He could have been going to work.

"What a couple of old farts," she said.

"I guarantee there will be people onstage older than us."

"*There's* something to look forward to. Kidding. Just kidding, just kidding, justkidding, justkidding."

"Do I need to cut you off?"

"That's the problem, I'm sobering up."

"We can't have that." He moved to the living room and used the little key to open the minibar, stepped aside and presented its contents like Carol Merrill. "Your pleasure, milady?"

"They'll have drinks there, I'm assuming?"

"If you want to stand in line all night. Plus this is on the house."

"What kind of red wine is there?"

"Sutter Home."

"Ew, no. What else is there?"

There was a little of everything.

"Is there tequila?" she asked.

"Someone's getting serious."

"It's a rock concert, right?"

"Rock and roll."

"Hells yeah, rock and roll," she said. "Take that Jack too."

"I wasn't gonna leave it."

She watched him slip the miniature bottles into his socks. "What are we, in high school? You think they're gonna frisk us?"

"You never know."

"I can take a couple."

"Where you gonna put them?"

"I have my hiding places."

"I'm sure you do," he said, though it turned out to be an empty boast. Her slacks were too snug to fit a bottle in the pockets, and she wasn't wearing socks.

"I'd be a bad smuggler anyway," she said. "I'm too chicken. You're the criminal in the family."

"Thank you," he said.

"You know what I mean."

"I think I'm maxed out. I don't want these falling out while we're walking through the mall. Time to get our pregame on."

He twisted open a nip of Southern Comfort and handed it to her. "To rock and roll."

"Rock and roll," she said, and tipped it back. She'd forgotten the boozy sweetness, the way it coated her tongue and teeth like syrup. "We really are back in high school."

"Just for one night," he said, as if that might be fun, and for a moment, slowed by everything she'd had to drink, she thought, if offered, she might actually seize the opportunity to rewind to sixteen or seventeen and start over to avoid all of this—then remembered Emma and Jeremy. You couldn't relive your life, skipping the awful parts, without losing what made it worthwhile. You had to accept it as a whole—like the world, or the person you loved. With the Southern Comfort warming her, short-circuiting her thoughts, the idea seemed profound, and then as Art was leaving a note for the turndown service and she was checking to see if she had her room key, she dropped the stupid plastic card on the carpet so it bounced under the glass table. Recovering it required all of her faculties, and by the time she straightened up, clutching the arm of one chair like the rung of a ladder, the notion was gone, replaced by the urge to dance until she was sweaty and party till she didn't give a shit about anything.

Odds of Heart playing "Crazy on You" in concert:

  1 in 1

Even as they waited outside in the bright, sterile mall, shuffling toward the theater doors with the other latecomers— most of them their age, Art noted—the reek of burning weed was overpowering, and brazen. He'd forgotten it was legal here, or at least decriminalized. Marion sniffed the air and arched her eyebrows like Harpo.

Inside, a fog hung in the trusses overhead, reflecting the kaleidoscope of the light show, and he wondered how the owners got around the fire code. When a joint came down their row, she hit it and passed it to him as if it was natural. He held the smoke in his lungs, watching Nancy Wilson strumming her twelve-string and stepping forward to press a pedal, her skin tinted yellow and then red under the gels. Her hair was only shoulder-length, and straight, not the luxuriant tresses he remembered, and she was noticeably thin, as if she'd been sick, her wrists bony. Though he'd sworn it was her, the woman from the restaurant had been someone else. It wasn't the first time he'd gone out of his way to prove he was a fool. This was minor, comparatively. He exhaled, adding his breath to the cloud above. Beside him Marion swayed to the music, the crowd singing along so loudly he could barely pick out the vocals. It was like being trapped in a giant karaoke bar on Heart night.

For years he'd been hearing that dope was stronger. Now he believed it. They'd been drinking for hours, so maybe it was the combination. His lips were numb, his face a rigid mask, as if he were slowly being paralyzed. He felt himself receding, a flickering brain cell trapped inside a thick, inert head, like the lighted stage at the end of the dark auditorium. He watched the crowd as much as the band. They played two or three favorites, then a new tune nobody knew, everyone settling again, as if in protest. Someone down the row must have had a bag of joints, because they kept coming. The smell was piney, almost sweet. Marion coughed and laughed at herself, offered it to him. He needed to be in control for the dry run later, and rather than abstain and look like a lightweight, he took in a shallow mouthful and blew it out.

The new tune garnered tepid applause, and then the stage— the whole place—went black, as if they'd lost power, only the red exit signs floating in space. In the dark, people shrieked and whooped and whistled, called out songs. After a long minute a single orange spot found Nancy Wilson downstage, perched on the very edge, one high-heeled boot atop a monitor, her right hand raised straight in the air like Pete Townshend about to windmill. She waited until the shouting and catcalls subsided, lowered the pick to her Stratocaster and broke into the galloping opening riff of "Barracuda," making everyone jump up.

She played it twice, three times, torquing the whammy bar, bending the last jangling chord so it ricocheted off the walls and scattered, then spun, kicked, and the flash pots bloomed like fireworks, blinding, as the rest of the band jumped in, thunderous, hitting them like a wind. *So, this ain't the end, I saw you again*, Ann shrilled. Marion grabbed him, and though he had no idea how to dance to the song beyond a headbanging pogo, and understood they looked as ridiculous as all the stiff, middle-aged baby boomers around them, he tried to match her enthusiasm, sticking out his chin and pouting, Jagger-like, lip-syncing to the words he didn't know he knew. Her smirk was a challenge, half put-down, half come-on. They mock-taunted each other with the chorus. *And if the real thing don't do the trick— no?—you better make up something quick. You're gonna burn burn burn burn burn to the wii-iick*. The coda was all churning guitars and flashing strobes. After the last cymbals crashed and the lights died, they embraced, sweaty, celebrating the greatness of the song and how wasted they were. When she kissed him, he tasted weed and tequila. She hung on his neck, shouted in his ear, "Is there anything left to drink?"

He made it his mission. There was no sense in both of them going. His mouth was dry and he had a craving for a beer anyway.

As he'd predicted, the lines were endless, the concessions people painfully, irritatingly slow. He didn't mind missing a couple of cheesy power ballads from the eighties, but while he was still a dozen people from the front, he recognized, from a lifetime of AOR radio, the fingerpicked flamenco intro and then the strummed buildup giving way to the big fuzzy falling-down-the-stairs riff—"Crazy on You." *We may still have time, we might still get by*. The song could have been about them, and he wished he were there with her for it.

Part of the reason the line was so slow was that they had to check everyone's ID, which made no sense, given the crowd. He shifted from foot to foot, looked to the ceiling for patience. The waiting was giving him a headache, and then when he reached the counter, incredibly, all they had was light beer, they were ten dollars apiece, and he could only buy two.

He didn't tip his server, then felt guilty, which pissed him off even more. He took a sip from each beer so they wouldn't spill and hustled across the concourse, skirting the steady stream leaving the arena. The band was playing another new song no one cared about. As he made his way down the aisle, he passed dozens of people texting on their glowing cellphones.

Back at the seats, Marion was doubled over, her head twisted, one cheek pressed against the seat in front of her. A woman he'd never seen before knelt beside her, shining a flashlight app around like she was trying to help. He thought Marion had passed out, and blamed himself for leaving her, and then she straightened up, smiling goofily, pinching something tiny and glinting between her fingers. The woman cupped a palm to receive it, tilted her head and refastened her earring. "Oh my God, thank you so much," she said, hugging Marion like a long-lost friend. They were both completely stoned. She was from the row ahead of them, and bumped him as she slipped past, nearly spilling the beers.

"You were gone awhile," Marion said, taking hers.

"I heard 'Crazy on You.' What else did I miss?"

"Nothing too exciting."

"All they had was Bud Light."

"That's fine."

It was a waste. By the next song, his beer was gone. Marion swayed along to "Alone," but for him the mood was ruined. His back hurt from standing. It had to be nine-thirty. No way they would go two hours. He counted the songs they'd played, thinking they must almost be done. He imagined they were saving "Magic Man" for the encore. As they ran through their later, lesser hits, he expected every song to be the last. He pictured the casino teeming with people, the blackjack dealers calmly revealing their hands, servers bustling between tables with free drinks.

Between songs, as Nancy was switching guitars in the darkness, Ann strode to the front of the stage.

"We know it's not Valentine's Day, but we're not here tomorrow—sorry. So we'd like to wish everybody a happy Valentine's Day, all right? All right. This is a special night, and Niagara Falls is a special place, so before our last song we'd like to bring two people up here for something special." She checked her cheat sheet. "Please welcome Tom Rutkowski and Alison Spagnotta—I hope I got that right. Tom here has something he wants to ask Alison."

The crowd cheered as the couple walked on, and for a moment Art felt as if he'd been robbed. He rubbed a hand over the bump in his pocket to make sure the box was still there. Why hadn't he thought of it? It seemed obvious now. A simple phone call and they could have been up there instead of these two—hefty, even beside Ann Wilson, and weirdly familiar. As the man lowered himself to one knee, knightlike, in the spotlight, Art recognized the orange Harley bandanna and leather vest.

"Holy crap. You know who that is?"

"Who?" Marion said.

"They were sitting right across from us on the bus."

"Yikes. Don't remind me of that bus."

The woman said yes, and the couple embraced to a standing ovation. A gracious hostess, Ann Wilson kissed them each on the cheek and sent them off, waving to their new fans. As the lights dimmed, then died, Art imagined the congratulations awaiting them, and the happy place this memory would have in their married life, and thought that once again, through his own lack of imagination or foresight, he'd blown another chance.

From the darkness, softly, lilted a synthesizer riff he associated with something bobbing in water, and behind it, revolving like the scratchy edge of a record, the crash and hiss of surf washing ashore. Gradually the lights came up, bathing the stage a marine blue. A guitar joined in, and another synth, their twinned, single notes descending slowly, sweetly. He knew the song but couldn't quite place it in their catalog—because it wasn't one of theirs, he realized before Ann sang a word. It was the Who's "Love Reign O'er Me," disorienting here, a complete surprise. As a teen he'd been skeptical of the anthem, too inexperienced and self-conscious to buy the idea. Now, on the far side of romance, he wasn't sure it was realistic, or was he unworthy of the sentiment, split as he'd been? It made him think of Wendy and the beach, the lunch hours they'd sat at the chained-down picnic tables, necking and planning a future that never happened.

Marion tugged at his arm, and he leaned down. "I love this song! I didn't know they played this song."

"They don't," he shouted. "It's probably because it's Valentine's Day."

He wasn't sure she heard him, because she didn't respond, just swayed by his side as Ann overpowered Roger Daltrey.

At the end, both Wilson sisters came forward, arms over each other's shoulders. "Thank you," Nancy said. "And good night," Ann said. They bowed and threw a *Dating Game* kiss. "We love you!" The stage went black, the synthesizer riff and the crashing waves still circling, softer and softer, until they were lost in applause.

All around him people held up their phones, a ghostly phenomenon he'd only seen on commercials and disliked on principle. The few surviving smokers raised real lighters, blatantly violating the law. He wished he had one.

They clapped in rhythm—"We want Heart! We want Heart!"

As expected, the band returned for an encore, taking their places again. Cynically, he thought it was all choreographed, as slick and shallow as Vegas. Why did it bother him? Everyone sold out to survive. It was the price of getting old. He'd tried his best, just no one was interested.

They surprised him with another cover, Led Zeppelin's "Rock and Roll," which he danced to, feeling faintly embarrassed while Marion flung her hair around. *Been a long time since I rock and ro-olled.* It was true. He had no moves, and was already pondering which of the two tables they should play. He bopped along, nodding in time, but finally gave up during "Magic Man," standing quietly beside her, constrained and impatient, as if waiting to be released.

Odds of a black number coming up in roulette (European):

   1 in 2.06

   Maybe what she needed all along was to get stoned, because walking through the high-stakes tables of the Lord Stanley Club, surrounded by players losing thousands of dollars every second, the whole place seemed unbelievably, laughably fake, and for the first time since Art unveiled the plan, she thought she saw the logic of his thinking. The money wasn't real, so why not have some fun with it? It was like Monte Carlo night at church, a riskless thrill for the timid, which, despite what he might say, included both of them. They would have never been there if they hadn't already lost everything.

   Unlike the wide-open, gaudily decorated galleries downstairs, the club was a high-ceilinged room the size of a private library, separated from the main floor by an imposing black marble reception desk and paneled in what appeared to be teak. The atmosphere was serious, even stuffy. There were no slot machines plinking, no hidden speakers blaring classic rock, no revolving LED screens promoting the in-house restaurants and shows. The entryway might have been a stage set. Below a full-length portrait of Lord Stanley himself, a fireplace lined with river stone blazed, attended by a pair of substantial wingback chairs. The design aspired to an exclusive businessman's club, a civilized retreat, except for the baize-topped tables jammed with older, chain-smoking Asian men in suits. At a glance, she understood that she and Art were the foreigners here.

She was also certain that everyone knew she was stoned. When a server came by offering champagne, she took one from the tray and quaffed it, both for cover and to settle her nerves.

There were no open seats at either of the two roulette wheels, and rather than forfeit whatever slight advantage Art thought they would have here, they waited, sipping and dispassionately watching the action, as if they might learn something from it. The croupier looked Chinese as well, possibly Korean, a husky pie-faced guy with a brush cut who kept the wheel lazily spinning while the players placed their bets. He plucked the ivory ball from the winning slot and, backhanded, sent it zipping around the rim, its orbit magically resisting decay—magnets, she suspected. The players reached across one another, adding impulsive last-second bets, pushing him stacks of chips to put on the numbers at the head of the table.

"Pick a number," Art said.

"Seventeen." Emma's birthday.

"I'll take thirty-one." Jeremy's. "How much you want to put on it?"

"How much do we have?"

"Right now, a thousand."

"Five hundred," she said.

"Look at you, going big."

They didn't actually bet, they were just passing the time till they could get a seat. It was more fun with something to root for, even if it was imaginary.

The croupier rubbed his palms together and silently passed a hand over the board, preventing any further betting, and by some hidden mechanism the ball dropped, spiraling down around the banked, polished bowl and across the circling numbers until with a woody knock it struck the raised gates of the tray, popped up onto the bowl and rolled down again, clattering from slot to slot until it finally lost all energy and settled. From where they stood, she could see only half the wheel, and had to wait till it came around—now just a passenger along for the ride—to see the ball had landed on 17.

She squeezed his arm. "How much would that be?"

He looked up, as if watching his brain do the multiplication. "Straight up, thirty-five to one, that would be seventeen thousand five hundred dollars."

"*Scheisse.*"

"Minus the five hundred I lost."

"Seventeen thousand."

"Pick a number," he said.

"Why?"

"To prove it wasn't just beginner's luck."

"Okay—twenty-three."

It didn't hit. Neither did any of the other numbers they chose, no matter how intently she focused her mind powers. It was a fluke, as random as the wheel. They were doomed to lose, to be taken by the house like the pigeons they were.

And yet the players at the table were winning, the croupier counting out stacks of different-colored chips after each spin. It was the same at the other table, where a pierced loudmouth in a hipster's stingy brim was crowing, "It's all skill, baby." No one played just one number straight up. They played five or six at a time, and the white lines and four corners between numbers, hedging their bets. The most common strategy seemed to be to haphazardly scatter your chips to cover as many numbers and combinations as possible, rather than Art's plan of simply playing black, except, as they waited, she noticed some of the winners were actually getting back less than what they'd put down, the odds gradually wearing away their stakes.

That was what happened to a wizened, slick-haired man to their right wearing bifocals with one dark lens. Down to his last stack, he bet everything and lost. He nodded as if he'd expected it, gathered his empty glass and napkin, and, without a word, stood and offered her his seat.

"You ready?" Art asked.

"No, you go. Show me how it's done."

He'd brought a single thousand-dollar chip, which he slid across the table. Before the croupier could make change, a server—also Chinese, slim and miniskirted—appeared to take their order.

Art deferred to Marion.

"Some champagne?" she asked, as if it might not be available.

"The same, please," he said, trying his best to be debonair, which she thought hilarious.

He received a hundred maroon-edged chips, ten stacks of ten, five of which he set aside before he made his first bet—twenty dollars on black.

"Minimum bet is fifty dollars," the croupier reminded the

table at large, and Art added three more chips. He sat back while the other players craned over the board, loading up the few unclaimed numbers until only 19 red remained, her eyes naturally drawn to the empty square. As the croupier waved his hand to close the betting, she weighed the possibility that the wheel was fixed. It didn't have to be, she reasoned, but was still relieved when the ball came to rest on 11 black.

She patted Art's shoulder. The croupier balanced a clear plastic cylinder atop the chips on the winning number and with both hands raked the losers into a hole before doling out the winnings. Art kept the stack he gave him and let the fifty ride.

He lost the next one, and doubled his bet. The server returned with their champagne—drier than her first glass—and she realized she'd been so engrossed in the game that she'd forgotten how wasted she was. She thought it was the anxiety of having money on the table. Just watching him, she was jittery, her blood riled up. She didn't think she'd care so much. From the beginning she'd thought it was a crazy idea; now each time the ball dropped, she was pulling for him to win.

34 red came up, then the green zero, the house number skunking everyone.

He kept doubling on black, as if it had to hit eventually. She could see the adrenaline working on him too. As soon as he lost, he grabbed another stack, impatient to get the next bet down— fifty this time, as if he'd given up on his plan. She wanted to lean in and tell him to mix things up, to bet on red, or bet more, spread it around, but stood quietly behind him. As if to prove her point, the man beside him hit big on 5 red, hauling in a dozen stacks of yellows topped with a trio of brightly striped thousand-dollar chips he casually pocketed—and then a few spins later won again and cashed out, tipping the croupier a hundred.

"I guess this is the lucky seat," she said, taking the empty chair.

"It's not mine," Art said. "That's for sure."

Their server appeared to see if she needed a refill.

"How about a Jack and Coke?"

"Better make mine a double," Art said.

She started with the minimum. She didn't bet with or against him, going instead for a mix of straight numbers, splits and corners. She had a piece of the winner, 33 black, and earned back her stake plus thirty dollars.

"Nicely done," he said.

"Nicely done yourself."

"I just needed you here."

"Aww."

They both lost, then, incredibly, she won again, a split this time, collecting an impressive double stack just as the server delivered their drinks. They toasted each other, the whisky, like the Coke, sweet and immediate, making her think how strange it was, after all their careful budgeting and Sunday coupon-clipping, to be tossing around money like it was a game. Yet instead of terrifying, their recklessness was weirdly exhilarating, like the fights they'd waged over Wendy Daigle, elemental, all pretense of normal life abolished, the false past gone, the future purely uncertain. She could see why people became addicted to the feeling, throwing away their savings chasing the high not of money but of sheer possibility.

She used some of her winnings to cover more numbers, hoping for a big score, but lost when 16 red came up. The next spin they both lost, then one of her corners won, another red. She noticed that having her own chips on the table relegated Art's winning or losing to an afterthought, which, if unavoidable, felt wrong.

He needed a win to replenish his bank. She offered him a hundred but he declined, putting the last of his chips on black. He won, staving off the inevitable, then lost as she hit 27 red straight up for three hundred fifty dollars.

"Well done."

"It's all luck," she said with a shrug, yet arranging her stacks in front of her gave her immense satisfaction.

Again, she offered him a hundred. This time he accepted. He lost again, and still he put his last fifty on black.

"I should be doing better than this," he said.

"Should be like a wood bee."

"That zero screwed me."

The croupier passed his hand over the board. The ball rattled and hopped, stopping on 5 red.

"Jesus," he said. "That *just* came up."

She'd lost too. She offered him another hundred.

"No, you go ahead. The universe is definitely against me." He pushed back and stood, took his empty glass and pointed to hers. "Want something else?"

"Another one of these?"

He scanned the room for the server, then headed off toward the bar. He was trying to be a good loser, but this was supposed to be his game, and she could see his pride was hurt. She hadn't meant to show him up. She'd wanted him to win as much as he did, maybe more. For a moment she wondered if she should purposely lose the next couple to make him feel better. It would be easy enough. All she had to do was put a few hundred on a number and it would disappear. *I don't know what happened*, she'd say when he got back, *I guess my luck turned*. She could hear him saying it was okay, his sympathy masking secret relief, but when it came time to bet, she forgot him completely. She rose from her seat and reached across the board, greedily covering whatever looked good to her.

Odds of a couple making love on Valentine's Day:

1 in 1.4

He wouldn't have believed it if he hadn't been standing right behind her, counting the payouts. In less than an hour, following no logical system whatsoever, she won well over six thousand dollars. He hadn't done badly. With a larger stake, which he'd have tomorrow, he could see the Martingale method would work, it just took patience and the nerve to lose big. It was actually better that she'd won.

They celebrated at the bar of the Lord Stanley Club, toasting her luck with shots of Patrón, then weaved their way back to the elevators, leaning on each other. He'd left a ten for the turndown service, so there was chilled champagne waiting for them. The cork bounced off the ceiling and disappeared, the mouth foaming over, making her shriek. Halfway through the bottle, he ordered another of the good stuff and tipped the room service guy a twenty. Tonight of all nights they could afford it.

He hadn't seen her this silly since Mardi Gras, before the children were born. She scattered handfuls of chips on the bed like petals and dove after them, bouncing a few over the edge, then lay still like a murder victim, arms outflung, her hair in her eyes. She hummed, content to lie there, then rolled off, crawled on her hands and knees to the door, climbed the frame and swung into the bathroom. A minute later he heard the jacuzzi

114

bubbling. Already she was shucking her clothes, teasing him with a glimpse of her nakedness.

"Bring my glass," she ordered. "And turn off the light."

He whipped his shirt over his head, the buttons scraping his face. His pants shackled his ankles. He toppled backwards onto the bed, kicking them free. When he stood up, he discovered a hundred-dollar chip stuck to his butt and brushed it off. On his way past the dresser he snatched her rose, saw the vase going over but couldn't stop. He listened but didn't hear it break behind him.

In the corner of the tub, a single candle flickered. For safety it was fake, battery-powered, casting a pale glow like moonlight over her shoulders. Behind her, the window was steamed, the Falls a red blur.

"My rose." She stretched toward him to take it, and then her glass, her breasts wallowing, nosing the surface before she sat back. "I love my rose."

He was cold, and there was no graceful way to get in. He sat backwards on the lip to swing his legs over, but misjudged and slipped, bumping his hip on the edge of the seat.

"Watch out now," she said. "You okay?"

"I'm great."

He sank up to his neck, the heat enveloping him, entering his skin. The feeling of near-weightlessness was strange but pleasant, his penis bobbing free. He slid in beside her, thigh-to-thigh, his forehead already sweating.

"It's hot."

"It feels good." She turned to look out the window, rubbed a circle in the fog. "I think it's snowing."

He twisted to see, his knee pressing against hers, his free hand finding her side, fitting the curve of her ribs. It was coming down gently, scattered flakes drifting through the light cast by the windows above, then continuing invisible in the blackness.

."Don't tickle."

"I'm not." He slid his hand up, cupping the knob of her shoulder.

"This is nice," she said sleepily.

"Mmh."

He resisted the urge to touch her breast, afraid of ruining the mood. Normally he had to negotiate his approach, reading her every gesture as preemptive, a hedge against rejection, but as she turned from the window, in a move that seemed premeditated, she set her glass and her rose on the ledge, reached both arms over his shoulders and kissed him, her mouth warm and winey. They necked in the heat, blindly, lushly, clutching each other. She tugged at him under the water. He hooked his fingers between her legs, kneading her open, a different slipperiness. She climbed astride him, rocking, giving him one breast and then the other, driving down on him, arching and tipping her head back.

Though he rose to it, her desire surprised him, reminding him of Wendy and their frantic couplings, a slide show he immediately closed. Maybe this was Marion's way of reclaiming him, or maybe she was just drunk, her inhibitions overcome by appetite. He didn't care what the reason was. Like the strength of her ardor, or her surprising beauty in the wan light, it was finally beside the point. What mattered was that he loved her and she wanted him.

From behind him came a muffled thud. Another, and quickly another.

Above him, she stopped, distracted by something outside the window. "Cool."

"What?"

"Fireworks. Hang on." Before he could protest, she popped off of him. She knelt on the seat facing the window and bent over, presenting her curved, pillowy ass, reached back between her legs and guided him in. "Now you can see."

"Yes I can."

"You're rude," she said, amused.

"No, you are."

Below, distorted by the humidity, a red spider bloomed above the gorge, its legs spreading from the center, then fading to embers.

"It must be midnight," he said. "You know what that means."

"What?"

He reached over her back and dangled her rose in front of her. "It's Valentine's Day."

"I didn't get you anything."

"I've got everything I need right here."

"So do I," she said. "Actually, I could use a little more champagne."

"Take mine."

She was so casual, the trappings of the situation so close to porn that he wasn't sure if they were making love or fucking. He wasn't used to her talking, or drinking, and the angle was awkward, the bottom of the tub slippery. He had to squat, a position that hurt his hip, and the air was cold, the sloshing and slapping distracting, besides the iffy hygiene of the thing, the water a broth of secretions. In the window he could see the dark ghost of himself laboring, and from reflex pictured Wendy, the table in the hotel that was almost but not quite the right height, and the mirror that let them watch each other, the red garter belt she wore for him with the little silver clips, the cheap yellow roses from Kroger's on the nightstand. His mind was slow from the long night of partying, but he was alert enough to grit his teeth and resist the intrusion, fending off the familiar creep of regret and self-hatred. After twenty years, he had practice at it. He concentrated on Marion's skin, his hands at her waist, gratefully accepting what he knew he didn't deserve.

Odds of being served breakfast in bed on
    Valentine's Day:

      1 in 4

She woke up naked and dry-mouthed, wondering what had happened to her nightgown. Raising her head was painful so she lay still. A bath towel was tangled in the covers. Beside her, Art was rolling out of bed, making the mattress dip. The room was dark, the curtains leaking daylight. Far away, someone was knocking. Had they forgotten to put the stupid sign on the door?

"Tell them to go away," she said, one arm shielding her face.

"I got it." He groped in the closet for a bathrobe, rattling the hangers, then on the way out banged into something solid. "*Mother.*"

She groaned in protest before asking if he was okay—too late, he was gone.

She heard him talking to someone, the door closing, the bolt clacking home.

She expected he'd come right back, except he was taking forever. She closed her eyes and let go and was drifting off again, reentering her dream of their backyard with the weirdly spherical lemon trees and the blue jay with Karen's voice that had something to tell her, when the clangor of dropped silverware rang like an alarm.

"Jesus." Just the effort to speak hurt her head.

A minute later, Art appeared in the doorway bearing a tray with a rose in a vase, bringing with him the nauseating smell of sausage and coffee. "Did someone order breakfast?"

"No."

"Apparently someone did last night, because we've got a lot of it."

She didn't remember, and didn't care. "What time is it?"

"Nine-thirty."

He lurked like a butler, attending her. His eagerness reminded her of the children on Mother's Day, so pleased with their own offerings.

"Really?" she asked, but understood there was no point. "I guess I'll sleep when we get home."

He took this as an invitation, smiling and coming around to her side.

She wasn't going to have him watch her eat half-naked. "Have you seen my nightgown anywhere?"

He set the tray on the dresser and opened the curtains to the view, making her shade her eyes. It was bleak out but the reflection off the snow was blinding. Her nightgown was hanging on the door right where she'd left it yesterday.

Sitting up made her dizzy, the gyroscope in her head spinning. Scattered across the floor with her clothes from last night were dozens of chips. On the nightstand stood an empty champagne glass, foam dried to the sides. She remembered doing tequila shots in the bar, licking salt and biting into limes, then getting on the elevator. After that, everything was a guess. The towel meant they'd probably been in the hot tub, and done what drunk couples did. She wasn't surprised or ashamed, just tired. One more mistake she'd have to undo.

"Please stop staring." Tenting the top sheet like a poncho, she yanked on her nightgown. She was sure she looked awful, her hair flattened, last night's mascara a raccoon mask.

"You look beautiful to me."

"Yeah, no. Just let me complain, okay?"

The tray he set across her legs held a silver dish cover the size of a hubcap, a hole in the center exuding a buttery warmth. Ranked about it were the rose in its vase, a small coffeepot, a coffee cup on a saucer crowded with fake creamers, an oblong ramekin stuffed with sugar packets, a Bloody Mary in a water goblet, water in a water goblet, and a tin gravy boat of maple syrup covered in plastic wrap. He leaned in to give her a kiss. "Happy Valentine's Day."

"Thank you. Happy Valentine's Day."

He stayed by her side, expectant, as if there were more. All she was thinking of was the coffee, something to jump-start her.

"Aren't you eating?" she asked.

"I will."

Belatedly it came to her. He was waiting for her to lift the cover and reveal some thoughtful surprise—a gift, maybe: jewelry, or plane tickets. Whatever it was, they couldn't afford it. Like the chips they played with last night, it wouldn't be real, just a token, at bottom an apology for everything that had gone wrong. As he watched, she hooked a finger through the hole in the center and pulled the cover away.

The pancakes on the plate were heart-shaped, one overlapping the other, pierced by an arrowhead of sliced strawberries.

"Very nice," she said.

"I thought you'd like that."

"Are yours like this?"

"Actually we have four of them. I don't know why."

"I know why," she said. "We were wasted."

"Do you want bacon? We've got tons."

"Actually I'm not hungry at all. I'm just going to have coffee for now."

"Suit yourself. I'm starving."

He went to fix his own tray, and she poured herself a steaming cup, leaving room for cream and sugar. In the kitchenette, he was whistling. She considered the possibility of self-sabotage, a twisted pathology. She didn't want to give him false hope, just as she didn't want to crush him. The problem, she thought, was that it took so little to encourage him. They'd have to talk when they got home. For now, she renewed her vow to be more careful, promising herself she'd be stronger tonight, and then, as she was battling the stubborn foil tab of the creamer, she noticed, snug against her wedding band, in matching white gold, a diamond ring she swore she'd never seen before.

Odds of a jazz band playing "My Funny Valentine"
  on Valentine's Day:

  1 in 1

He didn't feel so great either, his head hollowed out, his throat a flue. Rather than complain, he took the opposite tack, overcompensating, tapping his competitive energy to rise above the fatigue and keep moving. It was their last day, and he was counting on the Falls to distract them from what was waiting later—mere hours away now.

After the slow start, he was afraid they wouldn't be able to fit everything in. At the same time he couldn't push her, and came up with what he thought was a less ambitious schedule, trimming the more far-flung attractions like the Whirlpool. They could walk across the Rainbow Bridge to the observation tower on the American side, have lunch on Goat Island, then come back and do Clifton Hill, and still have time to treat her to an hour or two at the day spa, a carrot he thought she'd appreciate.

"Two hours isn't enough to do anything. You need to be there all day. That's why they call it a day spa."

"I just thought you might like a manicure or something before dinner."

"You probably need an appointment."

"It said it was open to all hotel guests."

"It's Valentine's Day. I guarantee it's going to be packed."

They could always call down and find out, he was about to say, but kept quiet, not wanting to prolong the exchange. Obviously he was wrong, being ignorant of these things. He replaced the vase on the dresser, grabbed his glass and the heavy green bottle off the nightstand. They were neatening up for housekeeping, doing away with all traces of their celebration. On her hands and knees, Marion searched under the bed for any fugitive chips, and he wished he knew what the problem was. Last night she'd seemed happy with him. Yes, they'd been wasted, she especially, but he was of the school that drink revealed one's true feelings. When, in bed, he'd given her the ring, she said she'd never loved anyone but him and dissolved into tears, as if it were a new confession and not her usual grievance. Now he couldn't do anything right.

"I think that's all of them," she said, evening up the stacks on the dresser.

"Did you count them?"

"I can."

"Please."

While he was rinsing the glasses in the sink, she called, "Seventy-one seventy."

"You sure?"

"Count them yourself."

"No, it's just good to know what we've got to work with."

"We've got seventy-one seventy more than we had yesterday."

"Thank you."

He opened the closet and knelt at the safe, adding her

winnings to the packets of cash and other chips. Crammed into the small space it seemed a fortune, yet only reminded him of the magnitude of their debt. At the very least they needed to double their money and then hope the house sold.

"Can you put this in there for me?" she asked, holding out the velveteen box.

He looked to her for an explanation.

"It keeps falling off."

"Sure," he said, taking the box. "We'll have to get it resized."

"I think that's it for in here," she said, looking around the room. "Let me check Facebook real quick and I'll be ready to go."

"Take your time." Yet, setting the box in the safe, he was certain he'd gotten the size right. In his desk at home, in the back of his day planner, he had a page dedicated to her various sizes for just such purchases. She hadn't noticeably gained or lost weight, so he didn't know why it wouldn't fit. As far as he could recall, she hadn't said anything last night when they were splashing around in the tub.

As always, she took longer online than she said, describing Emma and Mark's big night out, then tapping away at a comment while he stood at the window, watching the gulls glide across the gray face of the cliffs opposite. It was windy, the column of mist decapitated, the flags on the plaza snapping.

"Might have to wear a hat," he said.

"What?"

"It looks windy."

"That's not what you said."

"I said we might have to wear our hats."

"You're ready to go," she said absently, as if it were ever a question. Her shortness reminded him of Jeremy's when he had to stop playing a video game to eat dinner, unwilling to give up the absorbing virtual world for the boring old real one. She clattered on for another minute, then, puffing up her cheeks and letting the air out, clapped her laptop shut. "Okay, here we go. Where are we going?"

"America."

"Been there," she said.

He counted leaving the room before noon a victory. The last thing he did was tuck the DO NOT DISTURB sign back inside.

They were hot in the hall, bundled up in their puffy jackets, and then, going down, the elevator stopped every other floor to let on couples dressed for a wedding. In the lobby, penned behind a fence of velvet ropes, a large party waited to one side of the chapel while another finished.

"I guess this is the day," he said.

"I guess so."

At the foot of the turnaround, a chauffeur in a cap and blazer smoked beside his idling limo. As they left the drive and turned down Murray Hill, the wind hit them, drawing tears from Art's eyes. Across the gorge, the Falls poured on noisily. With no sun, there was no rainbow, yet despite the low sky, traffic along the parkway was heavy, the usual throng clogging the plaza, taking pictures at the rail. As blustery as it was, being outside was a nice reminder that there was a world beyond the casino, and beyond themselves. From a hidden chimney came the savory smell of wood smoke, somehow reassuring, and still, he couldn't shake the fact that under her gloves she wasn't wearing the ring. Whatever was going on, she'd taken it. She couldn't ask him to take it back.

The walk was longer than it looked on the little pocket map. The whole way they could see the bridge in the distance, a tease. They passed beneath the Skylon Tower and beside a strand of park with a statue of Tesla posed atop half a turbine like a logroller, labored on past the Sheraton and the old casino, its barbered shrubs wrapped in burlap, and still they were no closer. She was dragging, and they stopped at a souvenir store for a bottle of water and to warm up, which only made going back out worse. He'd seen cabs, but they were nearly there. This far down, the crowd was thinner. It seemed they were the only people headed away from the Falls, as if they were going the wrong direction. A horse and buggy clopped past, the passengers swaddled in blankets.

"That's what we should have done," she said, sniffling behind her scarf.

"I bet the line's worse today."

"I'm going to have to pee soon. Just warning you."

"They should have some at customs."

"Shoulda woulda coulda."

The exit from Canada was like the unmanned entrance of a subway, a few turnstiles guarded by a surveillance camera. Above, catty-corner, an industrial heater racketed. They enjoyed the oily warmth for a moment before pushing through the doors and back into the wind.

Surprisingly there was no fence to keep them from leaping off, just a chest-high iron railing, leaving them completely exposed. They were the only pedestrians, a fact she commented on as if it were a bad thing. The lanes beside them were stopped, a train of buses and RVs. The view up the gorge took in not just all three Falls but the whole bowl, giving them a better perspective of the cliffs and the old powerhouse tucked above the near shore, the crazy scale of the ice bridge, directly below.

"Look at that," he said.

"It's pretty," she admitted.

As they trudged along, huddled against the cold, people in cars reached cameras out of windows to capture the panorama. He'd brought theirs, and popped off some shots of the gorge and the observation tower, a deck cantilevered from a massive pier like an aborted bridge, beneath which, like a dark veil, hung a safety net.

Halfway across, a wordy plaque marked the border. He wanted a shot of her with a foot in each country, but she relieved him of the camera and had him do it.

"I wasn't kidding about having to pee."

"It's not far," he promised, hoping they wouldn't have to wait in line.

He needn't have worried. There was a pair of restrooms right inside the doors.

"God bless America," she said.

Waiting for her with his jacket unzipped and passport in hand, he reviewed the possibility of doing things legally. Together they could bring in just under twenty thousand without declaring a cent. They could rent a safe-deposit box and empty it gradually, they just had to be careful not to get greedy. Valentine's and their anniversary would work perfectly. They could make it a tradition.

"It's interesting," she said, once they'd been processed. "There was a big metal amnesty barrel. I was dying to look inside and see what kind of goodies were in there, but there was a lock on it. Imagine the drugs, especially with all the seniors getting their prescriptions there. They probably have to empty it five times a day."

"I bet they get a fair amount of guns."

"What about money?"

He shrugged as if it hadn't crossed his mind.

"I wonder what they do with it all."

"Destroy it," he guessed.

"Not the money."

"I don't know, maybe they keep it. Maybe they funnel it back into the budget. Everyone's looking for new revenue streams."

The view from the American side was of the Canadian skyline, the futuristic sixties towers and bland seventies hotels, a testament to the perils of overdevelopment, doubly unfair, since the view from there was so pristine.

The line for the observation tower was worse than Journey Behind the Falls.

"Sorry," Marion said, "I'm not doing that. I did that yesterday."

"I agree. Let's go see the Falls. Are you hungry at all?"

"I need something."

They followed the roar to Prospect Point, and stood at the rail, watching the choppy river turn smooth and sea-green before spilling over the lip. Its chilly grandeur was familiar. During his childhood and well into his teenage years, the broadcast day had ended with a patriotic montage including a black-and-white clip from this vantage backed by a crackly rendition of "The Star-Spangled Banner," a signal that he'd stayed up too late and would regret it the next morning, yet there was a lonely pleasure in it too, knowing you were awake when the rest of the world was sleeping, a quietude as well as a sense of being closer, truer to yourself.

Sweet, false nostalgia, with its insistence on innocence and loss, brought him back to the prospect of amnesty. What, from his past, would he get rid of, if he could?

The obvious, though the idea of erasing those days was like disowning himself. He'd grown so used to running those afternoons over and over in his mind like beloved old movies, anticipating his favorite scenes—pathetic, yet whenever he and Marion weren't getting along, he retreated into these daydreams as if they still had substance, the ultimate result of which, after so long, was that he himself had less.

What could he do with the past but renounce it? It was worthless in the present—worse, a negative—and made him feel foolish and weak.

"Had enough?" she asked.

"Let's see if we can get someone to take our picture."

"Again?"

"Again," he said.

The nearest person was a stout Middle Eastern woman in a fur coat with Jackie O sunglasses and striped nails. He programmed the camera so all she had to do was press the button.

"Take two, please."

"Two?"

"One's enough," Marion said.

"Two." He held up two fingers.

He was glad he asked, because while the woman was framing them, another couple stepped between them, ruining the first shot. In the second, Marion was wearing her patient smile, her arm around his waist.

"Is good?" the woman asked.

"It's good," he said, giving her a thumbs-up. "Thank you."

"What was with the thumb?" Marion asked when they'd headed upstream.

"I was communicating."

"She spoke English."

"It never hurts to reinforce a compliment."

"Like: *You are something else*," she said, giving him a thumbs-up.

He doffed an invisible top hat. "Why thank you."

The Cave of the Winds complex was shuttered for the winter, meaning the only place to eat on Goat Island was the Top of the Falls Restaurant. They were serving a prix fixe Valentine's brunch, complete with a tinkling jazz trio, but the entryway was wall-to-wall with people holding their coats. The hostess said the wait for a table could be forty minutes to an hour, if they wanted to put their name on the list.

"I'm not waiting an hour," Marion said.

"Can we eat at the bar?" he tried, a long shot.

"Please, feel free, if you can find a seat."

Since it cost nothing, he had her add their name to the list, then cruised the room, expecting to get shut out. They'd have to leave the park to find anything, a good twenty-minute hike.

As if he'd planned it, another couple was just pushing back their stools. He and Marion swooped in, unchallenged. It was like stealing. They were on the far side of the bar, giving them a view of the trio grooving away in the corner, and the curved picture window looking out on the Falls. The harried barmaid left them menus and a wine list and hustled off.

"I'm thinking champagne," he said.

"I'm thinking a nap."

"That can be arranged."

"It's already one-thirty. When's dinner?"

"There's time."

"And you want to do your wax museum."

'We don't have to do anything. We've got the whole day to ourselves."

"I don't mind the wax museum, I just don't want to spend all day there."

"I'll be quick," he said. "Promise. Boom boom, in and out."

"I've heard that before."

The brunch came with champagne, an out-of-season raspberry in each flute sending up bubbles. She slid hers over to him.

" 'A man who says no to champagne says no to life,' " he quoted with a bad French accent.

"You want me to puke?"

"No."

"Then just say thank you."

"Thank you," he said, toasting her.

His first glass cured his headache; the second made the place seem ideal. After a cappuccino and some banana bread, she revived, laughing at the picture of them by the edge.

"What a puss. Gimme."

"No way. This one's going on Facebook."

They were warm, eating eggs Benedict and listening to a blue "My Funny Valentine," while outside, the mist boiled up and gulls kited on the wind. The crowd in the entryway had overflowed, a few couples taking their cue, standing behind the line of stools, waiting for someone to leave. There was no rush. Soon enough they'd have to venture out into the cold again and start the long march back to Canada, but for now, if only temporarily, he was happy right where they were.

Odds of a married woman having an affair:

1 in 3

Clifton Hill was a glitzy strip of fast-food joints and silly, overpriced attractions the children would have loved twenty years ago and that Art, with his fondness for corndogs and miniature golf, still considered fun. She'd never been fun, and the blister on her heel had popped halfway across the bridge, making the dinosaur statues and haunted houses and fudge shops less whimsical than irritating. GET LOST! the Mystery Maze tempted. She wished she could. She had no interest in laser tag or 4-D IMAX rides or indoor skydiving. The street smelled of frying grease, and all about them, vying for attention with teenybopper pop songs, speakers broadcast roars and screams and spooky laughter. Neon burned as if it were nighttime, the yellow bulbs on the Movieland Wax Museum's marquee racing maniacally around the edges like falling dominoes. She thought they would stop there but he kept going, climbing past Ruby Tuesday's and the Great Canadian Midway arcade and the gigantic SkyWheel and the Rainforest Café and the mysteriously named Boston Pizza, toward the crest of the hill, where a block-long model of the Empire State Building lay tipped on its side, King Kong perched on top, gripping its antenna and snarling down at them with unfocused, totemic rage—Ripley's Believe It or Not! Museum.

"Wow," Art said, "it's completely different," stopping on the corner to get a picture.

"I'm not sure I see the connection. And I don't remember King Kong knocking it over."

"It's not supposed to make sense."

"Then it succeeded."

He fanned out a handful of coupons.

"I thought you wanted to go to Madame Tussaud's."

"I don't think we have time to do both if we want to fit a nap in."

"It's totally up to you." He'd already promised. She wasn't going to bargain with him.

"I think this looks more interesting overall."

"Okay then."

As they were crossing the street, Art stayed her arm. "Check it out."

On the sidewalk below the glaring Kong, the biker couple from last night stood toe-to-toe, jaws thrust forward, yelling at each other, oblivious to the passing foot traffic openly gawking at them. The woman was crying with her arms crossed tightly over her chest, the man shaking his head.

"I don't *care* about them, I just want *you* to be happy with it," the man argued, palms up, as if he were offering her a deal.

"Well you already ruined that with your stupid fucking remark."

"I said I was sorry! What do you want me to do?"

"Yikes," Art said when they were safely inside. "What do you think happened?"

"Obviously it was his fault."

"And they were so happy."

"Welcome to married life," she said.

"That's right. No free passes."

You got one, she could have said, but there were people around. She felt grubby enough just overhearing someone else air their private feelings. She and Karen had had to be so careful, not wanting to become a target of break-room gossip. Every little resentment they squirreled away grew and festered separately and then came spilling out when they finally had a chance to talk, all of them related to the main issue, the impossibility of the situation, which would never change, no matter how much they discussed it. Maybe that's what they'd needed, a big cleansing blowup instead of the endless analysis and tortuous recriminations. At least when she and Art had fought, they'd fought honestly. There was no need to think before she spoke, no pretense of softening the blows, even if, afterward, she wished she could take back some of the crueler things she said. She thought she understood the couple on the street. Better that complete release than a bitter impasse. It was a good lesson to remember.

There was no line to buy tickets. After waiting all day yesterday, she took it as a bad sign. In a far corner of the lobby, between the coat check and the restrooms, a padded bench ran along one wall. Her blister stung. Her head throbbed. All she wanted to do was sit down, but he'd be hurt if she didn't go with him, as if it were a criticism or coldness on her part. She accepted the admission sticker he gave her, declined the brochure and followed him in.

The first gallery was dedicated to primitive rites. A row of wax busts illustrated tribal body modifications—distended lips, necks and earlobes—an interactive map on the wall highlighting the country of origin at the touch of a button. Art said he recognized one of the shrunken heads from last time, which she thought was impossible. She could barely recall being there. The ceremonial daggers and fertility symbols and blowguns whittled from thighbones were generic, a mix of the macabre and exotic geared to children, who made up the bulk of the audience, dragging their parents from one display to another, having their pictures taken inside a sarcophagus or astride the world's smallest horse. Little was original, let alone authentic. In smudged plexiglas boxes sat priceless artifacts of the ancient world, shiny with varnish. Most of the exhibits were simply reproductions of old wire service photos. Several times, waiting for him to read the notes on the wall, she had to cover a yawn.

The next room housed, on one side, a massive collection of swords, and on the other, medieval instruments of torture. Behind ropes, a diorama worthy of a chamber of horrors depicted the Spanish Inquisition, a prisoner stretched on a rack while his glassy-eyed captor touched a red-hot poker to his stomach. The tip of the poker glowed like a nightlight.

"Funny *and* true," she said, and still he read every word.

They saw a carrot shaped like a hand. They saw a Statue of Liberty made of Necco wafers. They saw a fifty-foot tapeworm fished from a Samoan woman's stomach. They saw Cleopatra's false teeth and a faint hologram of Abraham Lincoln reciting the Gettysburg Address. Art especially liked the collection of bullet-stopping pocket Bibles that had saved soldiers from the First World War all the way through Afghanistan. Pictures were encouraged, a yellow-and-red Kodak symbol on the wall prompting visitors as if on their own they might not recognize the opportunity to commemorate their moment with the six-legged calf or the world's tallest man's Chippendale chair, or, in Art's case, the Buddha made of over three million dollars' worth of shredded bills.

Like the little girl before him, he rubbed its belly.

"Here," he said, "I'll take a shot of you."

"You forget, I'm already lucky."

"Come on. Today we need all the luck we can get."

Knowing he wouldn't let it go, she gave in. The Buddha was surprisingly cold, the compressed money like stone. What was she supposed to wish for—that they'd lose? Posing, she feared the camera would expose her ambivalence, and tried to smile.

The feeling pursued her through the next few rooms, more unsettling than the fakirs and contortionists and the woman struck by lightning nine times. Conveniently, she'd put off thinking of last night and the ring, the same selective amnesia she'd practiced when she was with Karen, temporarily burying her unhappy secret only to have it resurface with an ache. Having been so easily betrayed, she hated being dishonest. Plus, as Celia often noted, even over the phone she was a terrible liar. After her impatience with the cheesiness of the museum, she was relieved that he had something other than her to focus on, and was glad to sit down in the darkness of the Robert Ripley Theater and put on the oversized 3-D glasses like a mask.

The seats were cushy, and reclined.

"Wake me up if I snore," she said.

The screen went white, revealing a few people sitting toward the front. One coughed, his head bobbing, and the room went black. From the sound system insidiously rigged beneath each seat came a rumbling that seemed to grow from within, as if it might split her organs, and then, with a crash, they were at the edge of the Falls, the water turning green and going over, triumphal travelogue horns trumping the roar as the crane swung up and back to show the whole glittering vista. The 3-D effect was more striking in a treetop helicopter shot, flashing down the rapids and sailing weightless out over the gorge, but it seemed ridiculous to be sitting inside watching when right outside they could see the real thing.

The subject of the film wasn't the Falls but the daredevils who hoped to become rich and famous using them as a stage. What looked like actual footage sketched in the history. The narrator might have been Donald Sutherland. The first to come were the tightrope walkers. Despite the tricky winds, simply walking across soon proved too tame, forcing them to cook up more elaborate stunts. To breakneck ragtime, in jerky fast-motion, an acrobat pedaled a bike across a wire—forwards, backwards, then again with a frilly assistant on his shoulders, twirling a parasol— amazing yet so effortless as to be uninteresting. It didn't seem possible, but of the dozens of tightrope walkers who'd defied the mighty Niagara, not a single one had died—"Believe it or not."

"Believe it," she stage-whispered.

There were no such guarantees with the eccentrics who

designed their own barrels, which made their attempts more dramatic, waiting to see if they'd make it, and why, but the glasses hurt her eyes and she closed them, picturing herself sitting there in the theater, the light playing over her face. She and Karen had never gone to the movies. They met for drinks after work at an out of the way Chili's, and then, when there was no longer any reason to pretend they were just friends, at Karen's, where they held hands on her lumpy futon and talked about her girlfriend's deployment and how screwed up everything was. Marion had never been with a woman, and after some initial awkwardness was surprised at how natural it felt, how right, yet occasionally after they made love, Karen would get upset over some little thing and end up sobbing and angry, saying this was exactly what she didn't want to happen and that they had to stop. Because Marion needed to be home to cook dinner, their time was brief, and usually these breakdowns took place as she was getting herself together to leave, making the transition back to the other world and the other person she was that much harder. Instead of feeling doubly wanted or torn, she only felt more alone. She wondered how he'd done it for so long. In a twisted way, she envied—in retrospect—how effortlessly he'd carried his secret, and then, when it grew too heavy for him, confessed, unburdening himself by dumping it on her. She was tempted to repay him, but in the beginning Karen had made it clear their arrangement was temporary and that Marion wasn't the first, an admission she should have heeded as a warning. As impossible as it seemed now, she'd thought she was in love, or maybe after his passion for Wendy Daigle, she just wanted to be. Even before they stopped meeting after work, she had to concede the affair had been, in every sense, a disaster. When they finally broke it off, she was left with an empty secret, one she expected she would take to her grave.

"Hey." Art poked her shoulder. "You awake?"

"Just resting my eyes."

They were inside an echoing steel barrel like a space capsule, looking out a porthole, the pitching rapids spinning them, making the crowd groan as if they were seasick. A jagged rock loomed in 3-D, and they banged off it, jarring the frame. They surged past the old scow and the powerhouse, gaining speed, whitewater sloshing all around them, the sky tilting crazily. Ahead, the railing at Table Rock bristled with sightseers, a rainbow rising out of the mist. The sound system rumbled, vibrating up her spine. On the verge, as they were about to go over, he reached across the armrest and laid a hand on her leg, as he habitually did during the final preparations before takeoff. She thought he might be making fun of himself, or the film, since there was nothing to fear, and so no need for reassurance. At the same time she couldn't ignore it, and rather than give him a reason to doubt her, she covered his hand, patting it as if to say they'd be fine.

Odds of a lover proposing on Valentine's Day:

   1 in 17

     Outside, the wind had picked up and the clouds lowered, making it seem colder. The day was almost gone—Sunday, with its promise of solace and rest, a fleeting respite from the week. After the cab ride back they didn't feel like going anywhere. The lobby jangled like a pachinko parlor, driving them upstairs. Housekeeping had renewed the room, leaving fresh roses, a box of truffles and a stuffed chimp holding out a heart embroidered with WILD ABOUT YOU, which he hoped would soften her and which she accepted with open yet gentle skepticism, noting that he hadn't actually chosen it himself.

     "If you don't mind," she said, "I think I'm going to go lie down."

     "Is there a certain time you want me to wake you up?"

     "I need an hour to get ready for dinner, so whenever that is."

     They'd been together all day, and were ready for some alone time. Art took a water from the minibar, sank into the couch and turned on the Olympics, while she retired to the bedroom and traded her clothes for a hotel robe. There were too many mirrors in the bathroom, providing her with unflattering views. She peeled away the flap of dead skin on her heel, leaving a stinging oval the color of raw pork. She had some Neosporin in her bag and was dabbing on a thin coating when her phone rang, a quick trill to let her know she had a Facebook message.

Usually it was nothing pressing, distant friends posting something amusing on her wall, a forwarded YouTube video or a link to a site they thought she might like. She saved them to go through at night, sitting with her laptop on her knees like a heating pad while they watched TV. Art gave her grief, saying she was addicted, but it was just another way to pass the time, and more interesting than his PBS shows. And it could be useful, like now. The message was from Emma. It said: *ANSR YR FON!*

Though it hadn't rung since she'd turned it back on in the cab, she had two new voice messages. She hated AT&T.

The first was from Emma: "Hey Mama. It's Sunday, around three-thirty. You're probably out having fun. I'll try you later. Love you. Happy Valentine's Day."

The second was too, except now the background was a wash of noise: "Hey. It's four-fifteen. If you get this, give me a call on my cell. We're heading out and I really need to talk with you. Okay, bye."

The alarm clock/iPod dock on the nightstand said it was four thirty-five.

She sat on the edge of the bed to call.

The line rang, then rang again too soon, as if she might get sent to voicemail. A blip and Emma was saying, "–just because you lost. Stop. Hey, Mama. Sorry. We had a bet and someone's being a poor loser."

"What's up?"

"Didn't mean to interrupt your big romantic weekend."

"Unlikely. We were at the Ripley's Believe It or Not! Museum."

"Believe it or not."

"Exactly. Where are you? I can barely hear you."

She was being loud herself, attracting Art, who peeked in the door. *Emma*, she mouthed, pointing to the phone.

"I called because I wanted you to be the first to hear our big news."

"I had a feeling." She thought she knew what it was but didn't want to take the pleasure of delivering it away from her. They should have moved in together last June, except Mark's nana disapproved.

"Mark proposed."

She thought she'd misheard, but no. Proposed.

"Mom?"

"It's about time," she joked, to disguise her shock. Though Emma was twenty-seven, three years older than she'd been, her first reaction was that she was too young.

"What is it?" Art asked.

"Mark proposed."

"Congratulations, Bemmy!" he shouted.

"Did you hear that?" she asked.

"I heard. Thanks, Dad."

He sat on the bed, jostling her.

"Do *you* want to talk to her?"

"When you're done."

"And you accepted, I take it?" she asked.

"I did. We're heading over to his folks' place right now."

"Have you picked a date?"

"We haven't gotten that far. I'm still freaking out. It was a total surprise."

"Believe me, it's an even bigger surprise here. Congratulations. We're so happy for you. Tell Mark we don't care that he's a Steelers fan."

She asked after the ring and told Emma she loved her, and Mark too, that it was wonderful, they were absolutely thrilled, yet after handing the phone over to Art, she wondered how this would complicate things. How were they to share their love as parents but not otherwise? For all her daydreams of life on her own, practically she was unprepared. She had no plan, no strategy, just a vague and hopeful sense of freedom that involved only herself, making her fear it was imaginary.

When Art got off, he took her in his arms, his happiness precluding any dissent.

"It's the best Valentine's Day ever," he said.

"It's definitely a surprise."

"This calls for champagne."

"Later. If I don't get some rest I'm going to fall asleep at dinner."

"Want company?"

"I want to sleep. Go watch your thing."

Alone in bed, she felt like a traitor. It was partly his fault. Why did it annoy her that he would do anything to please her? In a way it was an imposition, an unfair demand. She thought she should call Celia but lacked the will. She left the drapes open, dusk drawing a curtain on the gray day, leaching the color from the room. On the dresser, her rose was black. In the dimness, the distressed armoire that housed the TV and the striped wallpaper and the tacked-up crown molding all seemed elaborate, needless fakery.

The bed was too hard, the pillows too spongy. She tried lying on her back. Directly above, a smoke alarm flickered red, ready, and she rolled over. In the hall, a lock clacked, a door opened and closed heavily. The elevator cables sang. She drifted, picturing Emma's wedding, a garden in June, white folding chairs ranked on a lawn, a program on each seat, bees meandering, lighting on purple irises, their legs sugared with pollen, and then she was in a vaulted train station in Paris, sometime in the past, like an old black-and-white romance, waving on the platform in a cute cloche and a trench coat, but whether she was meeting someone or saying goodbye, she couldn't say.

In the sitting room, he lay on the couch with his arms folded over his chest, the TV a bright square mirrored in the coffee table. He watched it on mute so as not to bother her. He cared nothing for cross-country skiing, lanky Scandinavians in bodysuits following doggedly in one another's tracks, but quickly found he was rooting, out of some warped principle, for the leader to fall.

Emma's news was welcome, a source of joy, except now he had to figure out how to pay for it. It would be too obvious if they waited till after the wedding to declare bankruptcy. He wished he'd known six months ago.

Simply, they had to win. Statistically, the Martingale method was sound, a classic negative progression. When they won, they'd bank their winnings and bet the same amount again. When they lost, they'd double the bet, and keep doubling it so that when they eventually won, they'd recover everything plus their original wager. Because eventually, with near even odds, they'd win. It was a question of patience and the willingness to lose big. Starting with forty thousand dollars, opening with a thousand-dollar bet and assuming they banked absolutely nothing, they'd have to lose five times in a row. He was betting that wouldn't happen. Most likely, somewhere in that sequence of five escalating bets, they'd win, recouping their losses and banking another thousand. The key was not being greedy and overreaching. It might take them five minutes to win that thousand dollars or half an hour, and they might have to risk thirty-one to do it, but the odds were overwhelmingly in their favor, and with each thousand they'd be that much closer to a sixth saving bet, making their odds even better.

As often as he reassured himself, after everything that had happened, he still harbored some doubts, the most troubling of which was that five wasn't a very large number. He wasn't deluded, as Marion thought. He understood that, though the odds favored them, they could easily lose. He acknowledged the possibility as he acknowledged his hangover or her disenchantment, preferring to put his energy into overcoming it.

All day he'd tried to be positive for her. Now the fatigue he'd held off settled on him. He welcomed it, tired of bearing their failures himself. Half a lifetime ago he'd made a series of complex and terrible decisions he deemed not simply necessary but urgent, vital to his happiness, his very existence in the world, yet which now seemed foolish and immature—desperate, ugly flail-ings under pressure. It was possible he was doing it again, just overcompensating the other way. He was afraid of letting her down again, or was it already too late? He didn't have the energy to pursue the thought. The couch was soft and warm, the skiers' clockwork striding hypnotic, and soon his eyes went unfocused, then closed, commercials flashing over him as, outside, night fell.

For a time, while they slept, the gorge lay invisible, a blank described by the lights around it, until, silently, all at once, as at the press of a button, the great banks of floodlights popped on, tinting the Falls and, faintly, their separate rooms, the color of love.

Odds of winning an Olympic gold medal:

  1 in 4,500,000

He was right to be afraid to wake her. Disorganized at the best of times, she hated being rushed and, flustered, turned on him. He knew she needed an hour. It wasn't her fault he fell asleep. She was sorry, they'd just have to be late.

He absorbed this ultimatum casually, as if it were no big deal, which further annoyed her. To underscore her point, she dawdled in the shower, letting the steam open her pores, only to discover, on getting out, that he'd called down and changed their reservation. He seemed pleased, as if he'd solved the problem. He understood nothing, though she couldn't say this without seeming unreasonable, and instead told him he could use a haircut.

"I know," he said. "It's on my list."

Besides having a jacuzzi, the bathroom was twice the size of theirs, and still they were incapable of sharing it. His timing had always been terrible. She sat on the bed in her bathrobe, waiting for him to finish shaving so she could dry her hair.

After thirty years he'd learned to rinse the sink.

"Do you want the ironing board out?"

Did he have to ask? And why now? "Do you need me to iron something for you?"

"Just a shirt."

"What about your pants?"

"I think they're okay."

"Gimme. I might as well do them while I've got it out."

He didn't resist, knowing it was futile. She did his things first, her hair wrapped in a towel, while he sat at the kitchen counter in his boxers. For years she'd wondered out loud why he couldn't just learn to iron, a mild complaint he'd come to agree with from sheer repetition yet never acted upon. He accepted that he was a burden on her. These moments of domestic helplessness were his penance and tribute.

"Thank you," he said, taking his pants.

"You're welcome."

He ceded the bathroom to her, using the mirror in the entry-way to tie his tie, a bright scarlet befitting the occasion. The suit was his best, last worn to a job interview that hadn't panned out, and he worried it might be unlucky. Too late.

She was still in her bathrobe, curling her hair, and he turned on the Olympics—the pairs figure skating, which she enjoyed.

"That's great," she said when he announced it, "but I can only do five things at once."

He couldn't sit down for fear of wrinkling his suit, and circled the room, stopping at the window and looking out over the American Falls and the city beyond, red lights blinking atop electrical towers marching off into darkness. Emma was getting married. The fact should have given him some extra perspective on what they were doing there, yet the connection eluded him. They'd have to tell her the truth, an eventuality he didn't dare contemplate. So much of being a parent was protecting one's children from one's own mistakes. That was the greatest failure, he thought. It shocked him now, but when he was with Wendy, he didn't care, he'd been willing to sacrifice everything.

The Russians' music was lush and brooding, dark strings and spooky woodwinds building to a crescendo, then a quiet passage, their skates scraping the ice as they set up for a jump. It seemed unfair that one slip could undo a lifetime of dedication, but there it was, the late takeoff and rotation, the awkward sprawl as the crowd gasped, and then, up again, the trouper's smile as she resumed the routine. They showed it in slow motion, the girl's painted face, so composed, opening in shock as she landed hard on her hip, an arm outflung. He needed a drink, and looked in to see if Marion wanted anything.

"I'm coming," she said, leaning over the sink to draw on eyeliner. He'd had to convince her to buy a new dress for tonight. The one she chose showed off her arms and shoulders, two of her best features.

"No rush. I like the dress."

"You just like the cleavage."

"I like the straps and the way the waist goes in."

"Stop. This isn't *Project Runway*."

"And the cleavage." He couldn't deny he'd peeked.

"It's old cleavage."

"It's always new to me."

"Now I know you're lying. What are you having?"

"Vodka. They've got the Citron."

"I'll take a white wine, I don't care what kind. Can you grab my jewelry out of the safe?"

He delivered her glass to her, then opened the closet and punched in the combination. The velvet box sat right beside her jewelry bag, and though he felt slighted, he left it there rather than press the issue.

She needed help with her freshwater pearls, a task he was happy to perform. She stood with her head bowed while he battled the tiny clasp, squinting like a surgeon. For his reward, he kissed her neck—warm and smelling of her moisturizer.

"Okay," she said, ducking away. "I'm trying to get dressed here."

She spritzed both sides of her throat with perfume, down her cleavage, and finally one wrist, rubbing it against the other as she headed for the bedroom.

"You have to stop following me," she said, and he retreated to the sitting room with his drink, swirling the ice cubes and watching the Falls. He thought of ordering champagne for later but didn't want to jinx things.

The Canadians were leading, and he wondered if it was rigged, since the games were in Vancouver.

She came in with a lace shawl over her shoulders and stopped as if posing for him. "Well?"

"You look great."

"No." She pointed to the floor. She was wearing two different shoes. "Which one?"

He'd faced this question hundreds of times and seldom got it right. The key was to be honest rather than try to outguess her. At least then when he was wrong he'd have his integrity.

The one on the left was dressy, crushed velvet with a high

heel, elaborate straps and a needle-nosed toe. She loved them but they killed her feet. The one on the right was plain, but much more comfortable.

"The right," he said.

"You really like that one better?"

"I do."

"You're so boring."

"You've got a blister, and the restaurant's at the end of the mall."

"You're right," she admitted, but when she returned from the bedroom she was in her stocking feet, the fancier pair dangling from one hand. "When else am I going to wear them? I'm just going to have to suffer."

"You said it, not me."

"How long do we have? I'm not putting them on till I absolutely have to."

"Five minutes. Before we get going, I'd like to get a picture of us."

"You haven't taken enough pictures today." She thought it was typical of him, wanting to commemorate their adventure. He'd already chosen where he wanted her to stand. She could see it being used against her in the future, but couldn't refuse him.

"You don't have to put your shoes on."

"I do if I don't want to look like a dwarf next to you."

They were too narrow, and crushed her toes, her bunions flaring with every step.

"Ow ow ow," she said, hobbling over and leaning against his shoulder.

"Are you going to make it?"

"I'm going to have to."

"This'll take five seconds," he promised.

He programmed the camera, set it on the counter and dashed back, draping his arm around her waist.

They waited, holding their poses. She felt her smile weakening, turning thin and insipid, and was just putting on another when the flash blinded her.

"Let me check it real quick," he said, and left her standing there.

"Well?"

He nodded, impressed. "It's a really nice picture."

"Can I sit down now?"

He came over to the sofa and showed her.

"Wow," she said, because he was right. Her smile was genuine, and the dress flattered her. The flash and her makeup subtracted a decade, and for once her hair did what it was supposed to do. He was handsome and trim in his suit, his shoulders back, the gray at his temples giving him the air of a judge or ambassador. They might be broke and unhappy but even she had to admit they made a good-looking couple.

Odds of a couple fighting on Valentine's Day:

   1 in 5

     The mall was long and busy with window shoppers, and several times they had to stop to let her feet rest, making them late, and then when they finally arrived, they discovered there must have been some miscommunication, because the restaurant had given away their window table. She could see him struggling with the injustice of it. He had the printout from home in his jacket and unfolded it like a deed. The maître d' apologized, nodding and calling him sir, but there was nothing he could do.

     The room was curved and stepped like an amphitheater facing the Falls. A server ushered them through the other diners and sat them in the very center of the second tier, where they had a perfect view.

     "Well that sucked," he said.

     "This is nice."

     "Why did I even bother asking then? It makes no sense."

     "I'm sure they didn't do it on purpose."

     "I don't care if it was on purpose or not, it's not right."

     "If you're that upset about it, we can leave."

     "No," he muttered.

     "Then stop bitching."

"I'm just saying it's not right."

"It's not helping—that's what I'm saying."

"Move forward."

"Exactly."

"Suck it up."

As if prearranged, a different server brought a bottle of champagne, presenting the label for inspection.

"We didn't order that."

"Compliments of the house, with our apologies."

"Well, that's very nice. Thank you."

"Just what we need," she said, but it was true. After the first glass, the problem with the table was forgotten. While she was glad to have it behind them, it also bothered her how easily they could be bought off.

The room was dark to highlight the view. They strained to read the menu by the lone votive burning between them, tilting the pages sideways. She had to admit, he knew her tastes. It was her kind of place, the dishes rich and finicky. The black truffle beet salad appealed to her, and the scallop sashimi, and the pork cheek, and the lobster risotto with Pernod and fennel. She scrutinized the prices, knowing they couldn't afford it.

"Emma's getting married," he said.

"I still have to call Celia. I wonder if she's told Jeremy."

"I'm sure she has. What are you thinking of getting?"

"The risotto's speaking to me."

"I looked at that. I'm leaning toward the scallops."

"*Yes*—I wanted that too. Get it and we'll share."

"Remember the place on Captiva that made those scallops—"

"With the plantains. Oh my God that was good. What was the name of the place?"

"Sweet Melissa's."

"How do you remember that?"

Of all their trips, it was his favorite, a reminder of how they could be. "That was the night the rental car had a flat and we had to fix it in the dark."

"I remember."

The next morning they'd taken the ferry over to Cabbage Key to have a Cheeseburger in Paradise. He was about to recall for her the pod of dolphins that raced alongside the rail, surging ahead to leap the bow wave like teenagers playing chicken, when the server intruded, asking if they'd like something from the bar.

"We're fine with the champagne, thanks."

"Will you be having wine with dinner?"

"We will," Marion volunteered.

"I'll need a few minutes," he said, because he hadn't looked.

The list had the heft of a bestseller. As he leafed through it, following down the columns, the prices grew more and more ridiculous. He was tempted to order their most expensive vintage but wasn't sure his card could handle it. He chose a high-end Puligny-Montrachet, only to be told they were out of it at the moment, the same for a Meursault. His struggles attracted the sommelier, who pointed out the surprisingly few white Burgundies they had on hand. Art went with his recommendation, a lesser Meursault, more than he'd ever paid for a bottle of wine, yet somehow a letdown.

"That was difficult," she said.

"Nothing's easy today." It was a slip, which he quickly covered, saying the champagne was very good, hoping she didn't notice the non sequitur.

She did, but let it pass, agreeing with him, content to sip and watch the Falls and the couples around them, each, like themselves, in their own small circle of light. Several of the women had roses, and she wished she'd thought to bring hers. She was more comfortable with the rose as the badge of their love, being both natural and ephemeral, than the ring, which seemed binding and permanent, a claim on her. She could leave the rose behind and still recall its beauty fondly. She'd apply the same philosophy to tonight, taking in its pleasures, knowing they were fleeting. When was the next time she'd eat at a place like this?

They did their best not to fill up on bread, though the focaccia was delicious, still warm, with a hint of rosemary. Before their appetizers arrived, they drained the champagne and started on the white. She wondered if he should be drinking so much, but didn't want to ruin the mood by casting ahead. Instead, she matched him glass for glass, and found it made conversation easier. When there was a lag, the Falls provided a reliable diversion. The nightly light show had begun, the colors changing, lurid purples and sulfurous yellows tinting the mist. The food was brilliant. When they switched plates, they each said the other's was better. If it were a first date, she would have said it was a great success.

After their dishes had been cleared, as they were examining the spots on the tablecloth to determine who'd spilled more, a smattering of applause from above caught their attention—another proposal. They joined the tail end, clapping politely for the lucky couple.

"They're everywhere," she said.

"They certainly are." He didn't say that was exactly what he'd been planning to do, or ask what she thought he was doing last night. Nothing could be less romantic than that discussion, or more fraught, and they were having a nice time. Likewise, he set aside the apology he was going to offer for having to resort to the divorce. None of it was as important as being here, sharing this occasion with her, and, emboldened by the wine and his own sentimentality, he reached across the table and took her hand.

"You know I love you."

"I know," she said, then looked up, because the server had returned.

They broke, sat back to let him comb the crumbs from the table with a straightedge.

Were they interested in dessert?

"It won't hurt to look." From her smirk he knew he'd read her correctly.

"I'd like some coffee," she said, prompting a back-and-forth about how she wanted it, and did he want some as well, and by the time the server left them alone again, the moment had gone cold.

"You were saying," she said, and reached out her hand for him to take.

"I was saying I love you."

"And you know I love you. Whatever happens."

This last phrase was so important for her to communicate to him that she never suspected he might misinterpret it.

"Happy Valentine's Day," they toasted, and, believing at heart they'd been heard and understood, they were both happy.

Odds of the Cleveland Indians winning the World Series:

1 in 25,000

"I apologize in advance for the smell," she said in the elevator, steadying herself against him to take her shoes off.

"I don't smell anything," he said, but he always said that. His idea of gallantry was ignoring her shortcomings, which only drew more attention to them.

Luckily the hall was empty, the carpet cool and yielding beneath her feet. He had to swipe the key twice. When they were inside, she sat on the sofa and kneaded her toes. She was tired and wanted the day to be over.

"Call your sister," he called from the bathroom.

"Thank you." She didn't want to talk to anyone right now, but later would be even worse, and dutifully she fished her phone from her purse and pulled up the number. She half hoped she'd be out, but the last time they spoke Celia had made a big deal about not having any Valentine's plans, and before the third ring she picked up.

"What's up? I didn't expect to hear from you. How's the big romantic weekend going?"

"Good—actually *very* good on that front. Are you sitting down?"

"What?"

"Emma's getting married."

The silence was gratifying. "I knew it."

"You did not."

"Are you kidding? It was obvious at Christmas."

As Celia laid out her evidence, Art came in with his Indians bag and gently set it on the coffee table. Deliberate as a magician, he unzipped the zipper, removed two banded packets of bills and stacked them facing her. He tipped the bag on end, dredging up handfuls of chips, the plastic clattering, making her wave at him to stop. He continued gingerly, trying to be quiet, and she stood and padded to the window, listening to Celia reel off the clues she'd missed.

"Diamond earrings? Hello?"

"I knew they were serious. I'm just worried they're skipping some important steps. How do you know someone if you haven't lived with them?" After everything—and Celia knew almost everything—Marion understood how absurd it sounded, coming from her.

"You're asking the wrong person," Celia said.

"Maybe it doesn't matter." A figure flitted across the window, and she turned to see Art taking the bag back to the bedroom. He was ready, his nerves making him impatient. On the table sat four neat stacks of ten and a shorter stack she recognized as her winnings from last night. If they were going to risk everything, then these were hers to lose. She'd earned them. She bent down, making a claw of one hand, plucked up her stack and slipped the chips into her purse.

"How are *you* doing?" Celia asked.

"Okay," she said, as he returned to his place at the table. "I won seven thousand at roulette last night."

"What? How?"

"I'm a natural. Who knew? Listen, I have to run. We have to go break the bank." She promised she'd talk to her later in the week, when they could actually talk.

"How's she doing?" he asked, but only as a preface. He pointed to the empty spot in front of him. "I thought we'd add your seven to what we've already got."

"That wasn't part of the original plan."

"It's an opportunity. If everything goes well at the beginning, we can use it to do something big later on."

"And if everything goes wrong?"

"If everything goes wrong at the beginning, nothing's going to help us."

"So you only need it later, if everything's going okay."

"Right," he said, but hedging, as if it were a question.

"Do you mind if I hang on to it? I'll have it right here. It'll make me feel better to have something to hold on to."

"That's fine. You know you're going to be betting too. I'm not doing this all by myself. Besides, you've got the hot hand."

It was the first she'd heard of this, and she wondered if he was trying to placate or to implicate her. Changing the money was bad enough. She'd just assumed she'd stand there and watch him, free of any responsibility. She assumed he'd lose, and while that complicity made her uneasy, she accepted it, as she accepted her part in their marriage being a failure. Actively helping him would be a kind of sabotage, a self-admission that this was what she'd wanted all along. A better person would have never let it get this far. A better person would have been honest with him. A better person wouldn't have put on her comfy shoes before grabbing the cash and heading downstairs.

Odds of a divorced couple remarrying:

   1 in 20,480

    They waited for the elevator, but it refused to come, as if giving them a chance to reconsider. Though they both saw it as an omen, neither commented on it, not wanting to upset the other. The light was stuck on 3. He pushed the button again, as if that might do something.

    When it finally moved, it went down to 2, then M, then L.

    "All righty then," he said, and spun away.

    "Here it comes."

    Behind the doors, the cables whirred. The light blinked under the numbers.

    "Are you ready to play the feud?" he asked.

    "Are you?"

    "Survey says: I am."

    The car was empty. They dropped two floors before stopping, then just one, more people piling on, forcing them to the rear. The chips made the front of his suit lumpy, resting against his ribs. He felt like a terrorist carrying a bomb. She was his accomplice, their shared secret connecting them with every glance.

    She thought he was making eyes at her because somebody farted. Because somebody had. She touched the tip of her nose to show it wasn't her, a game Jeremy had brought back from college.

He did the same and made a face.

The Lord Stanley Club was on the mezzanine, but from habit he'd pushed L. They were trapped in the back, and rode down to the lobby, staying on when everyone else got off.

While they knew what was waiting for them, going from the artificial silence to the artificial din of the casino was like walking onto a factory floor. In vast, windowless rooms, row upon row of players sat tethered to plinking, flashing machines, impervious to the outside world. It might have been day or night, summer or winter. They might have been on Mars. All that mattered was the next bet, the next spin. The solitary ones haunted her, the older women, obvious regulars with their fanny packs and ashtrays. What kind of lives did they lead? Weren't there people who needed them? She imagined them going home to dark, empty apartments, something she secretly feared, the quiet evenings and weekends alone, hoping for a phone call from one of the children. Maybe that was why they came, for the life of the place, even if it was all a show.

"There's one," Art said, spotting a wall of cashiers' windows at the back of a gallery.

There was no line. She'd thought this moment would never come, as if his plan were a bluff, yet here she was, pulling the money out of her purse. It felt wrong, as if he'd tricked her, the whole scheme an elaborate con. Again, as she had since he'd hit on the plan, she thought it was her job to stop him, her evasion a betrayal, handing him—them—over to fate. Why hadn't she fought harder?

The banded bills were stiff. He stood aside like a bodyguard as she pushed the packets into the trough, accepted the handful of chips in return and signed the receipt.

"Feels weird, doesn't it?" he asked, adding the chips to the stash in his jacket.

She agreed mildly, mystified by his excitement. How could she tell him? It had felt like she was signing her life away.

They headed straight for the Lord Stanley Club, sweeping down the hall as if they were late for a dinner reservation. Her composure stirred him, and he was grateful. Now that they'd changed the last of the money, the hard part was over. He'd done the legwork and provided them with the best odds he could find. The rest was up to luck.

He'd start. Then if things went well, she'd spell him after a while.

"Remind me again," she said, "what's our strategy?"

"When you lose, you double the bet."

"What about when we win?"

"The bet stays the same. Just watch me."

"I will."

"The thing you have to watch out for is forgetting to double it, or doubling it too much." He'd had that problem when he was testing the system online, the repetition hypnotizing him. "You just have to keep track of your last bet. When I'm betting, you keep track, and vice versa. That way we've got a backup."

She didn't ask what she should do if she lost and kept on losing. She'd watch him. If they still had any money left after that, she'd figure it out.

The club was a haven of taste after the slot parlors.

"Welcome back," the ponytailed hostess at the black marble desk greeted them.

"Thank you," they said, as if they were members.

Something about the fire cheered him, and the oil portrait, the patrician air of privilege and ease, possibly, corny as it was. Who aspired to that hoary ideal anymore? He'd be happy enough paying his bills.

The place was just as busy as last night. Both roulette wheels were full. He marked the numbers that came up, but neither table went on a long streak. It was a shame: they'd be winning if he could only get a seat.

The ball stopped on 18 red.

"So now you double," she said, leaning in.

"Yup."

The ceremony of paying the winners took longer than she remembered. Finally the croupier lifted his plug and the players laid down their bets.

8 black hit.

"So we win four thousand," he whispered. "That covers the thousand we lost, the two we just bet, plus a thousand profit. That's how it works. No matter what we bet, every time we win, we make a thousand."

"And every time we lose?"

"Doesn't matter, unless we lose five times in a row. Then we're done. Then we go home. That's why I need that extra seven, to make the five in a row six in a row."

"Depending on how things go."

"Depending on how things go."

She discounted his certainty, based, as it was, entirely on theory. He could say with confidence that losing five times in a row was improbable, citing the odds, but what did he know about playing the game? Husbands and wives should love and honor each other, theoretically, till death, but that didn't always happen either. Planes crashed, banks failed, countries broke up. Since Wendy Daigle, she'd become aware of all that could go wrong, and his plan seemed reckless, doomed. He had no idea what he was risking. She wished she were braver. She wished, absurdly, for everyone at both tables to stay so he'd never be able to sit down.

He was worried they might have to stand there all night. These were the only high-stakes European wheels in the casino, and the players were serious, working with healthy piles. No one seemed to be losing. Maybe that was why a new croupier took over the wheel on the left, to cool the action. She was a squat bottled redhead with nubby fingers who looked like she should be replenishing the buffet. Intentionally or not, it took her a couple minutes to get settled. During the changeover, several seats opened up.

"Good luck," Marion said.

"Thank you."

She stood behind him with her hands on his chair as he unloaded his chips. The croupier counted them twice, watched by a pit boss, before giving him back the exact same number of yellows. While the other players mobbed the board, he took a single chip and put it on black.

The croupier brought her palms together, then waved a hand over the table.

The ball dropped, caromed, came to rest: 29 black.

Marion squeezed his shoulder, and he glanced back and nodded.

He set aside the chip the croupier slid him and let the first one ride.

While they waited for the other players to bet, he surreptitiously reached down and loosened his belt a notch. The chocolate mousse had been too much, on top of a heavy dinner, and now his gut was sending him distress signals. Some of it was nerves, which was understandable. While he'd worked in finance his entire life, money wasn't abstract to him. He was a collector of change, a clipper of coupons, a calculator of mortgage payments. If he felt a little sick, that was natural, but this was bad. It was just a matter of time before he'd have to find a bathroom.

The croupier closed the betting, and the ball dropped.

Zero won, the house number. Everyone but an older Chinese man with a pockmarked face lost. The chips clashed as the croupier swept them into the hole

Art shrugged and doubled up.

Easy come, Marion wanted to say, but stayed silent, afraid of drawing attention to them, the imposters. She thought her impersonation of a supportive wife was more successful. It fooled even herself. As much as she doubted the future, their hopes had been conjoined for so long, and their losses, that it was impossible not to root for him. As he waited for the wheel to stop, she felt the same helpless protectiveness as when she watched Jeremy playing basketball against bigger, more aggressive boys, so that when the number came up red, a pang of alarm shot through her.

He doubled up again, setting out four chips.

He wasn't worried. He'd faced this situation hundreds of times online. That was the beauty of the Martingale method. One win and all your losses were history.

Red again.

As the croupier paid the winners, he was aware of Marion behind him. The pit boss looked on like a cop. A cheer went up from the other table. One more and they'd be down to their last bet. He'd never lost this quickly on any website, and wondered for an instant if the wheel was rigged to foil the method. He rubbed one side of his face as if he were tired and raised the bet to eight thousand.

11 black won. They recovered everything, plus their profit. They were up two thousand now.

"Do you have any Tums in your purse?"

"Are you okay?"

"It feels like gas."

"I don't, sorry. Want me to get you some?"

"No," he said. "Yeah, would you? Maybe you can ask the girl at the desk."

Traitorous as it made her feel, she was relieved not to have to watch him. There was the Pepto-Bismol back at the room, but that seemed too far. The hostess said the closest place that might have something was the hotel gift shop, downstairs, right off the lobby.

The way back to the elevators seemed longer than she remembered, the galleries she passed through skewed and unfamiliar, as if she were stoned. No, there were her grandmothers with their fanny packs, still tapping away. She hustled along, her feet aching, all the while accusing herself of stalling. She pictured herself returning to find him at the bar, in shock, the whole ordeal over. It may have been a crazy scheme, she'd console him, but at least he'd tried. The larger question of what they should do could wait. There was a lot to talk about.

Downstairs, the lobby was lined with wedding guests waiting for yet another new bride and groom to emerge from the chapel. Instead of rice or birdseed, they clutched handfuls of confetti. Strangely, they all seemed to be speaking Italian. She skirted them, returning their smiles, and then when she was deciding between Pepto and Rolaids, heard the happy clamor. By the time she paid, they were outside, watching the limo off, the carpet drifted with the mess. In the elevator, she was surprised to find a red piece stuck to her shoe, as if she were somehow, if only glancingly, part of the celebration. She thought of Emma walking down the aisle, and then herself, younger, untried by life.

The happiest she'd ever been was with him, and the saddest. Was that the true test of love?

While she was gone, he began alternating his bets on red. The odds were the same, and it kept the wheel honest. As long as he doubled when he lost, it didn't matter. He plodded along, slowly padding their winnings, only once having to risk eight thousand. His stomach was worse, a cramp like a stitch making him wince and let out a breath. For a second he feared he was going to be sick. There were no empty seats, and he vetoed the idea of cashing out and going to the bathroom. The pain subsided, then returned, urgent. Between spins, he checked the entrance, expecting her, until finally he gave up, concentrating instead on the game. In all, he'd been there an hour and banked six thousand dollars. At this rate, to double their stake, they'd have to play till four in the morning. His stomach gurgled, and the man to his right turned to him, concerned, as if what he had might be catching.

She showed up in the middle of a spin with a roll of Rolaids.

"Take over," he said, getting up. "The bet's two thousand."

"Why's it on red?"

"The color doesn't matter."

As she sat down, the ball dropped. He stayed to watch.

They lost.

"So put four on whichever color you want."

"What color do you want?"

"It doesn't matter. Black, red, whatever. I've gotta go."

As she'd feared, he left her alone. She could see he was ill, but she also knew this was going to happen, that somehow she'd end up having to make decisions and bear responsibilities she didn't feel were hers. She took a sip of his drink and was disappointed to find it was plain Coke.

She put the four thousand on black, thinking he couldn't blame her for sticking with his original plan.

She won, and won the next one, banking the single chip. She lost a chip. She won two chips. She lost a chip. She was edgy yet bored, sitting there alone. It didn't feel like gambling, betting so mechanically. She wanted to cover the table like last night, play a half dozen numbers straight up with the high rollers. This way was only interesting when she lost, the anxiety of doubling up providing the missing thrill. And still, when she won, she won just the one chip, her victory incremental, and temporary, since one chip was the next bet. She'd thought he'd lost it when he'd come up with the plan, that the strain had made him desperate and deranged, but his strategy was exactly like him, methodical to a fault.

Win one, lose one, win two, lose one. It was a slow form of torture, and when he finally returned she was ready to give up her seat.

He was pale, and waved her down, shaking his head.

"That took a while."

"I don't think that was food poisoning you had the other night. I think it's some kind of bug."

"I'm sorry. It's no fun."

"Looks like you're doing all right."

"I don't want to be doing it at all," she said. "And definitely not by myself."

"Want me to take over? I can."

"Are you well enough?" She was going to suggest they quit while they were ahead, go home and start over, but obviously he wanted to continue.

"How much are we up?"

"Fourteen thousand."

"That's great. Add in last night and we're more than halfway there."

As encouraging as this was, she thought it was bad luck to mention it.

"Plus," he said, as if he'd forgotten, "two more and we get that sixth spin."

"Why don't you take over? I'm sorry, I don't have your patience. I'm ready to jump out of my skin here."

"What's the bet?" As always, his reasonableness shamed her.

"Two. Can I get you some water or something?"

"Please. That would be great."

She didn't need to know that he hadn't quite made it in the bathroom, so that immediately he had to move to another stall, or that it had been coming out both ends. He'd kept the second trio of Rolaids down, otherwise his stomach was empty, burning with juices. This was his one chance. He wouldn't miss it because of some stupid flu.

As if to rebuke him, the ball stopped on 0.

The man with the pitted face clucked in disgust and stood, defeated. The man beside Art took advantage of the extra room and slid down a seat.

She came back with his water and a white wine and sat beside him.

"I'm sorry, ma'am," the croupier said. "Seats are for players only."

"We're together," he said.

"That's fine as long as both of you are betting."

"Here," he said, giving Marion a chip to put on his.

They both won, meaning they both had to bet one the next time.

"I'm sorry, seats are for players only."

"For God's sake," Marion said, getting up. "There's nobody here."

She stood behind him, fuming, her frustration blooming into anger. When he lost, he asked her to sit, but she refused. Now she wanted him to win to teach the croupier a lesson, but the pace of the game and the nature of his strategy were against her. He won, but so little that it didn't matter. It was like watching someone play solitaire. She finished her wine and asked him to order another from the server. She expected the croupier to say beverages were for players only.

"Change these into fifties for her, please?" he asked the croupier, pushing two chips across the table. He patted the seat beside him. "Come on. Do what you did last night."

"What about your sixth spin?"

"Already got it."

The chips the croupier gave her were gray—a subtle dig, she thought. Four stacks of ten. She resisted the urge to blow them all on the first spin. She spread them around, craning over the table in an arabesque to place her bets rather than let the bitch touch them.

The contrast between her randomly scattered chips and his neatly centered one was too perfect, and made her laugh.

"What?"

"It's like a personality test."

"So what does that say about me?"

"You don't want to know."

They both lost, then both won when Emma's 17 came up.

"That's my girl!" she cried, for the croupier's benefit.

"Well done," he said

"How much is that?"

"That's going to be seventeen fifty."

"That's what I'm talking about!" She was just rubbing it in now.

"Minus whatever you put out."

"Still, not bad. Not bad at all."

She banked a thousand of her winnings and meted out the rest, covering most of the board, while he switched his single chip to red.

"Very bold of you."

He won. She hit a corner at 8 to 1, but didn't make back her stake.

"This redistribution of wealth is trickier than I thought," he said.

"Exactly."

Now that she was playing, he could stop worrying about her. They were close, only a few thousand away from doubling their money. His stomach was going to make it. He was amazed at how easy it had been. The method actually worked better than it did online.

When he lost the four thousand, he thought maybe he should stop, just cash in what they had, but she'd won, and with the slack they had, they could cover the eight thousand easily.

When they lost the eight thousand, there was no question they had to make it back.

When they lost the sixteen thousand, they were barely break-ing even. It was as if they hadn't won anything, as if they were starting over from zero.

The bet was thirty-two thousand on black. Or red.

This was what they'd come to do, yet now he doubted himself. They would have absolutely nothing.

He looked to her, half hoping she'd tell him to stop.

"First thought best thought," she said.

He chose black.

"Maximum bet is twenty-five thousand," the croupier said.

He'd researched the casino. It was a no-limit table, that was why they were there, but for a moment he thought she might be right, the rule might have changed. There was no sign posted.

"Can you please check on that for me?" It was because he was using a system, he was sure of it.

She conferred with the pit boss, who'd been lurking. The boss got on a walkie-talkie, then conferred with her again.

She came back over. "I'm sorry, sir. The limit is twenty-five thousand."

"Then I'll need to change these," Marion said, pulling a hand-ful of chips from her purse and spilling them on the table.

"Look at you," he said.

"Look at me."

"I guess we better win then."

"I guess we better."

The last five spins had come up red. The odds of this one coming up black were the same as any other, not quite even, thanks to the 0.

"Don't tell me that," she said.

"It doesn't change anything."

They held hands as the croupier waved a palm over the board. Behind her, the pit boss watched with his arms crossed.

She couldn't look, and bowed her head, pumping his hand like a blood pressure cuff. As with so many decisions in her life, she'd led with her heart, foolishly perhaps, unsure what she truly desired, just trusting in the rightness of the moment. If it was a mistake, she would have to live with it.

He knew what he wanted—what they'd once had, what he'd ruined out of selfishness. If she believed in him again, after everything, maybe he could too.

The ball dropped, hopping across the slots, kicking into the air, the gates batting it so it rolled up the bowl and down again, slowing as it skipped and clattered, nearly spent, bouncing out of 15 black and into 19 red, then onto the milled steel rim separating the numbers from their trays, its momentum ebbing, overtaken at last by the wheel's so that it wobbled along the divider like a drunken cyclist on a tightrope, their future together at the mercy of the smallest forces, until the ball teetered and dropped sideways, finally and decisively coming to rest with a pebbly click on 4 black.

"We won!" he cried, hugging her.

"We won!" she cried, hugging him.

But of course, they'd already won.

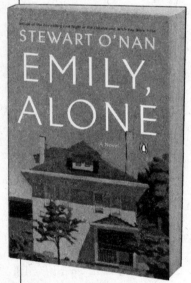

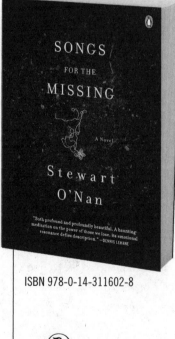

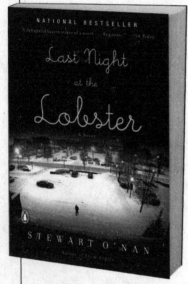